A SUMMONS TO GREYSTONE HALL

BY PERPETUA LANGLEY

Chapter One

Georgina drove her mare faster. Edmund was close behind her on his grey stallion, hoof-beats pounding through the crisp, morning air. Hyde Park flew by in a glorious green blur. Her mother would be scandalized to know that her daughter was just now galloping down Rotten Row, rather than sedately trotting the Ladies Mile. Still, Georgina never could resist a good horse race with her cousin.

A tight turn loomed just ahead. Georgina slowed her mare around the bend. After all, she could not win the race if she did not stay on the horse. She smiled at the thought of landing indecorously in the bushes, as she had done more than once before. Around the curve, a man on a black stallion suddenly appeared, cantering straight for her.

Georgina pulled on the reins and turned her horse, missing the oncoming rider by inches. Juno galloped off the path and narrowly avoided the trunk of an old oak tree. She patted her neck and said, "There, girl." Juno slowed to a trot and Georgina swung her around.

Her cousin Edmund had reined in his horse. Georgina thought he looked unaccountably annoyed. It was not like him to fall into a sulk. Nobody had been hurt – he should be laughing at her ridiculously close call. The man she'd nearly run over looked equally put out. Good Lord, they looked like a couple of old ladies.

Georgina trotted over to the pair. The man was on a sixteen hand stallion. He handled his horse with the experience that could only come from a lifelong habit of riding. He had ash blond hair and striking grey-blue eyes. Georgina thought they were rather like the color of a stormy sea. Particularly stormy at that moment. He would be quite handsome if he weren't glaring as if someone had challenged him to a duel.

Edmund nodded to the stranger. "Greystone," he said.

The man called Greystone seemed almost to be set in stone himself. Through tight lips, he said, "Carrington."

Georgina waited to be introduced to this cheerful person. Instead, he eyed her as if she were a housemaid, turned his horse and cantered down the path.

Georgina blushed. She supposed he thought her highly unladylike to be galloping down Rotten Row with a man in the early hours of the morning. Anger began its slow boil, like it always did when she was embarrassed.

"Who in the world was that?" she asked Edmund.

Edmund's dark eyes followed the man as he rode away. At the sound of Georgina's voice, he said, "Oh, him? Henry Greystone, the Earl of Knightsbridge."

"He must be the rudest man in England," Georgina said.

"Quite possibly," Edmund said.

"And so," Georgina said, wondering at how distracted Edmund seemed, "how do you know him?"

"Ah," Edmund said, softly, "from my club. Unpleasant fellow."

"I've never seen him before," Georgina said.

Edmund laughed and began to look like his usual cheery self. "No," he said, "you would not have. This is your first season, my girl, and the Earl just arrived in town three days ago."

"Well," she said, "I would not be sorry to never see him again."

"Prepare to be sorry, then," Edmund said. "His sister is hosting the ball you're attending this evening."

As Georgina trotted her horse back to the stables, she thought she really had better take her mother's advice and study Debrett's with a little more regularity. The ball was being hosted by the

Tennesby's. She knew her mother was great friends with Lord Tennesby's mother, the dowager. However, if Edmund hadn't mentioned it, she would have had no idea that Lady Tennesby, the hostess of the ball, was the married sister of the rude Lord Greystone.

There were so many new people to know! Not at all like the social life of Marksley Manor, where she could count on just five local families to provide amusement. Thank goodness her cousin Ann had agreed to come to London with her. Though Georgina put on a bold face, inside she had quaked at the prospect of all that had to be got through for her first season.

First, there had been the curtsy to the Queen, hoop skirt and ostrich feathers and all. Georgina had felt ridiculous in the outfit, though slightly less so when she found all the other young ladies dressed the same. She had mumbled something unintelligible to Queen Charlotte and backed out of the room as fast as she could. Then there was the ball to introduce Georgina and Ann to society. So many eyes staring at her for hours on end, by the close of it she had felt like a deer in a hunter's sights. Then there was the uncomfortable wait for the Almack's' voucher. Would they or would they not? Finally, the little cardboard voucher had arrived, and one for Ann, too.

Ann had said that she only received a voucher because Georgina's mother was old friends with Lady Castlereagh, but Georgina thought otherwise. Ann's steady good sense and calm demeanor impressed wherever she went. Georgina was not surprised the Patronesses had deemed to include her. The hard part of coming out was over and Georgina could not have survived it without dear Ann by her side.

It had taken hours of cajoling to convince Ann to come. It was almost a certainty that Sir Langston would ask for Ann's hand, but Georgina was determined that her cousin could do better than a local landed gentry. Ann was plain, so everyone said, though Georgina was prepared to do battle with anyone who suggested it to her. She did not bring much of a dowry, which was another strike. However, all who got to know Ann saw she was kind and good-humored and that intelligence radiated from her bright, brown eyes. That was how it was for Sir Langston, Georgina was sure – he got to know Ann and was smitten. Certainly the same could happen for her cousin in London.

Georgina bit her lip. Perhaps she should stop spending all her time planning Ann's future and start thinking about her own. Her mother had expectations that she would use the season wisely and come out of it betrothed. Georgina, on the other hand, had no such plan. She had heard from Clara Damesworth, a veteran going into her second season, that the second year was far more diverting than the first. In the second year, the first year jitters were gone and there were so many old friends to return to. That made perfect sense to Georgina, and she was determined to experience it herself. She knew what her mother would say about it – linger through the seasons too long and people will begin to think there is a reason for it. Georgina also knew what her mother was really worried about. She did not want Georgina to marry Edmund and had high hopes that the season would deliver up some respectable man that would take Edmund's place in Georgina's heart.

Georgina did not think her mother really understood her heart. How could she when Georgina did not understand it herself. She loved Edmund as a brother, yet there were times she thought she could fall in love with him as a husband. He was handsome, being tall and broad-shouldered with jet-black hair and dark eyes. Georgina had known Edmund since he was a boy and their temperaments were similar. She could imagine a life with him.

As Georgina had no brother, Edmund would inherit her father's estate and become Lord Marksley. Marriage to him would mean she would not have to leave her childhood home. On the face of it, it was a wonder that her mother was not scheming to make the match. It was as if Lady Marksley knew something about Edmund that she did not.

No matter, Georgina thought, handing Juno over to her groom. It was hardly worth worrying about whether she would accept Edmund if he asked, since he had not yet asked.

Georgina changed out of her riding habit and found her mother and Ann in the sitting room at Berkeley Square. It was her favorite room in the house, as Georgina found the rest of the rooms too large and drafty to be comfortable. The fire burned bright in the cozy room filled with comfortable, over-stuffed chairs and papered in a sunny yellow pattern. Her mother was just pouring tea.

"Ah Georgina," her mother said, "I presume you enjoyed your ride, your cheeks are blooming. It quite becomes you."

Georgina's mother, Lady Marksley, was a tall, elegant woman with blond hair and light hazel eyes. So different from Georgina's own raven-colored hair and dark blue eyes. Ann had once said that the difference between them was like a spring dawn and a blazing summer sunset. Georgina sometimes wished she had more of her mother's looks, just now blonds seemed to be all the fashion. Miss Stanhope and her blond curls had been the rage of last season, though Georgina had yet to set eyes on that divine creature.

Georgina pecked her mother's cheek. She thought it wise to omit the race down Rotten Row while describing her morning. "My ride was splendid," she said, taking a cup of tea from her mother. "And Ann, how did you occupy your morning?"

"How I spend most mornings," Ann said, with a mischievous smile. "Letter writing and entertaining callers."

Georgina sat at Ann's feet. "Of course you did, you perfect little person. While my very imperfect person just jumped on my horse and wasted away the time."

"You could take a lesson from your cousin, my dear," her mother said. "I'm quite sure you have a pile of unanswered letters hidden somewhere."

That was perfectly true, and Georgina felt guilty that she had let her correspondence slip. She knew all too well how it was to eagerly await news from friends in London.

"Oh come, Lady Marksley," Ann said, "let's not train the spirit out of our dear Georgina. Certainly her correspondents know that when they do finally receive a letter, it will be a lively account and well worth the wait."

"A little less spirit and liveliness would not be amiss," her mother said. "This is not the country. Remember, dear, that here your every move will be noted and talked about."

Georgina paled at that pronouncement. She wondered if Lord Greystone would see fit to spread it about that she had been racing her horse down Rotten Row with a gentleman. As she had not been introduced, the Earl could not know that Edmund was family. In any case, she was certain that racing her horse would not be approved of by the dragons at Almack's. How serious a crime had it been? Could they take back her voucher? Would she be labeled fast? She did not know.

From now on, Georgina decided, she would only be seen walking and trotting in Hyde Park.

It suddenly occurred to her that Lord Greystone had not bothered to get her name. Should he wish to spread the story he would not know who to accuse. Served him right.

"Georgina," Ann said, interrupting her thoughts, "whatever are you pondering? You seem quite far away."

"Oh, nothing in particular," she said.

"Further," her mother continued, "the Dowager Countess of Brantley called this morning. Very awkward that you were not here. If you must go riding, go in the afternoon like everybody else."

"Very well, mother," Georgina said. "Now, what shall I wear to Lady Tennesby's ball this evening?"

"Put on your best," her mother advised. "Lady Tennesby has a very eligible brother. I hear he is quite handsome."

"Lord Greystone?" Georgina said. "He's passable, I suppose."

"You know him?" her mother asked. "How did you forget to mention meeting one of the most sought after bachelors in England?"

Georgina colored. "Oh, no, we haven't been introduced. Edmund pointed him out to me."

Her mother frowned at the mention of Edmund. To get her mind off it, Georgina said, "Ann, what shall you wear? How about that divine pale blue silk?"

"Georgina, must you drag me to another ball?" Ann asked. "You know how tedious I find them."

"Do be a dear and go, Ann," Georgina's mother said. "The Dowager and I will no doubt sneak off to play cards as soon as we can manage it. Georgina will need a companion."

"Very well," Ann said, looking resigned.

Georgina hugged her. "You are the most divine person that ever lived. To show my gratitude, tomorrow morning I shall forgo my ride and stay with you, very sensibly writing letters and receiving callers."

At the mention of letters, Kingston brought in the post on a silver tray. "Ah," her mother said, taking the envelope from the tray, "Sir Langston has written."

At the mention of Sir Langston, Ann blushed deeply.

Georgina sighed. Her efforts at securing Ann a better match might well come to nothing. The two were terribly fond of each other. She did want Ann to be happy, but Georgina had been so hopeful that she and Ann would be able to keep houses in town. If that were to happen, they need never be parted for very long. Sir Langston was a good man, and respected in the county, but a house in town would likely be beyond his reach.

"He asks after you, Ann," Georgina's mother said, perusing the letter. "I shall tell him you are quite well."

"I suppose he does not remember to ask after me," Georgina said, laughing.

Ann smacked her hand. Her mother said, "Do not tease, Georgi."

Georgina held on to Ann's hand and kissed it. "I do not tease. Why should Sir Langston not be smitten with the most darling girl I know?"

Georgina had thought that she had said goodbye to her jittery nerves. She was out, properly launched, and the rest of the season should be all gaiety. Yet, getting ready for the Tennesby's ball, her nerves were back. It would be unlikely that she would be able to avoid seeing Lord Greystone. Surely he would attend his own sister's ball. But perhaps, Georgina thought hopefully, he was a gambler or had some other bad habit and would be off in some seedy neighborhood throwing his money away or consorting with loose women.

Georgina smiled at the thought of the grim-looking Earl of Knightsbridge carousing the streets. No, Greystone would be at the ball. But perhaps she made too much of the incident in the park. After all, she had just been riding and she had been accompanied by her cousin and two grooms. Perhaps riding a bit faster than would be quite right, but it was not as if she had done anything truly terrible.

Georgina decided to find out what Ann thought about it. Ann could always be trusted for sound, sensible advice.

Ann's room was a spacious bedroom that had been always reserved for her convenience. Lady Marksley had it specially decorated for Ann, since she was so often Georgina's companion. It was an airy room with pale blue paper on the walls and a thick carpet underfoot. Georgina noticed that it was as organized as always with not a ribbon out of place. Quite a different vision from her own room, which at times appeared as if a great storm had blown through. Her maid Jemma spent as much time putting things away as Georgina spent taking them out again.

Ann's maid, Fleur, was just finishing her hair. Ann's hair was naturally straight as a pin and Georgina guessed her maid had been fussing with the curling tongs for ages.

"Have you come to check on my uncooperative hair, Georgina?" Ann said, laughing.

"It looks darling," Georgina answered. In truth, it did. Ann's new maid was skilled.

"I would not go so far as to say darling," Ann said, "but I will say that Fleur knows how to make the most of what she's faced with."

Fleur blushed as she arranged the last curl.

"Now Georgina, tell me why you are in my bedchamber instead of in front of your own dressing mirror, getting ready for this most important ball," Ann said. "Remember, your mother mentioned that Lady Tennesby has an eligible brother."

Georgina sat on the bed and gazed at Ann's reflection in the mirror. "Yes, him," she said. "I've seen him."

"So you said. I believe you mentioned his looks were only passable."

Georgina blushed. "In truth, he is handsome. Quite so, but I do not like him one bit. What I failed to tell my mother was how it happened that I saw him. You see, Edmund and I were just having a friendly race down Rotten Row and, well, I nearly collided with the man."

Ann's face paled. "Georgina. Racing down Rotten Row? My brother is so irresponsible!"

Georgina felt that was unfair. After all, it was she that had suggested the race and galloped off. Edmund had just followed her.

"Now Ann," Georgina said, "it was not Edmund's fault. Truly it was not."

"It was," Ann said. "He was escorting you. As a male relation he has a responsibility to make sure that you do not…"

"Make sure I do not what?" Georgina asked. She was beginning to be terrified by how serious Ann looked.

"Georgina," Ann said. "You are naturally high-spirited. It is a wonderful quality, but yet a quality that could lead you to trouble. My brother should be ensuring that it does not."

Georgina twisted her diamond bracelet around her wrist. She'd had no idea that Ann viewed her temperament in such a light. Of course, Georgina knew she was high-spirited compared to other girls her age. She had certainly been told it enough times, in rather approving tones from her father, but less approving by her mother. Until that very moment, Georgina had felt it was one of her better qualities. She had thought it was a quality that Ann admired. Edmund was supposed to ensure she did not make a fool of herself! Was she really that silly?

Ann came and sat by her on the bed. "Come now," she said, taking Georgina's hand, "do not look so glum. I suppose Lord Greystone did not think too terribly much of it. You are certainly not the first girl to gallop through Hyde Park. What did he say?"

"He did not say anything," Georgina said softly. "He just looked at me and rode away."

"Oh my," Ann said. "He snubbed you?"

"Entirely," Georgina said. "He did not overlook me, he saw me and rode away without even a nod."

"That is unaccountable," Ann said. "Look at you! How does a man not acknowledge you? By the by, that gown suits you well."

Georgina glanced in the mirror. She wore one of her favorite gowns - a deep violet silk with a pale blue tulle overlay. Somehow, she did not think she looked as well in it as she usually did. "I look like the girl that was snubbed in Hyde Park by the Earl of Knightsbridge," Georgina said ruefully.

"And you were not doing anything else? Just Riding?"

"Nothing, except nearly running him over." Georgina smoothed her dark curls. "Though it seems to me that a gentleman should not be so shaken by a near miss with a female on a horse."

Ann thought for a moment. Then she said, "You are the daughter of Lord and Lady Marksley. Galloping a horse is not a crime and your near collision was merely an accident. Though I will thank goodness it was in the morning, as you would have been seen by all of London in the afternoon. As it is, aside from Lord Greystone, you were probably only observed by grooms out exercising their master's horses. You will enter the ball tonight with dignity. If Greystone brings up the subject, which I doubt he will, you will respond by commenting that you did not know who he was this morning, as you had not been introduced. That will turn his rudeness back on him and, if he's any sort of gentleman, that will be the end of it."

Georgina hugged Ann. "Dear girl! That is exactly it. We shall not run from the enemy, instead we shall mount an attack and charge the castle."

Chapter Two

Despite Georgina's plan to boldly charge the castle, she was uneasy as she entered the Tennesby's ball. She thought it was quite unaccountable that she felt herself in the wrong, simply because Lord Greystone had snubbed her. She had only been riding with her cousin, not murdering her maid. Georgina realized that this was the first time anyone had snubbed her, and it stung. She vowed she would never do it to anyone else, unless they really were murdering their maid.

Her father steered her toward Lord and Lady Tennesby and she vaguely heard Lady Tennesby say, "Charming." She did not know if that was in reference to her, or Ann, or her father. The ball was already crowded and hot, Lord and Lady Tennesby were popular hosts.

Ann squeezed her hand. Georgina gratefully squeezed back. If she must face Lord Greystone, and probably turn a hundred shades of red doing it, at least she had stalwart Ann by her side.

"Come General Georgina," Ann whispered, "time to storm the castle."

Georgina and Ann entered the throng of young ladies and gentleman in the ballroom. Lord Tansby, eldest son of the Duke of Rutland, was across the room. Georgina was sure he would ask her for the cotillion. She liked him immensely as he was a jolly fellow, and he was considered quite the catch, but she could not take him seriously with his bulging fish eyes. He always appeared to her as if he were running out of air.

Lord Tansby approached Georgina and Ann. He bowed and Georgina and Ann curtsied. He would be a respectable partner for the cotillion, Georgina thought. She had danced with him often and his conversation was always amusing.

"May I have the cotillion, Miss Carrington?"

Ann blushed. Georgina realized she was blushing too. Why had she just assumed Lord Tansby was coming to her and not Ann? He had spoken to Ann at other balls. Now that she thought about it, he had taken Ann in to supper at the last.

Lord Tansby led a stammering Ann away. Georgina suddenly felt utterly alone without Ann by her side. Good Lord, would she really sit through the opening set?

Georgina scolded herself to stop being so selfish. Lord Tansby might be just the thing for Ann and it would not kill her to sit through a dance. It would just feel like she had been killed.

She gazed around the ballroom like one did when they were desperately trying to appear unconcerned. Where on earth was her cousin Edmund? She always counted on him to be her dance partner in a pinch, but she hadn't seen him anywhere.

Ladies and gentleman were pairing up quickly. She scanned the first group of couples at the top of the ballroom and saw Lord

Greystone. His eyes met Georgina's and he quickly turned to his partner.

Was it possible to snub someone from across a ballroom? It certainly felt so. He had looked as if she was the most unpleasant sight he had ever seen. Of all the moments to note her – standing there alone like an idiot. Georgina felt the urge to run from the ballroom. She would like nothing better than to be in her own carriage, barreling home. She could crawl under the coverlet and forget Lady Tennesby and her awful brother ever existed.

"Miss Marksley?"

Georgina suddenly realized Mr. Simons, the son of a baron, was standing in front of her.

"May I have the dance?" he asked.

"Yes," Georgina said gratefully. As he led her to the floor, she felt as if she had been drowning in a lake of embarrassment and the kind Mr. Simons had just pulled her ashore. She had never liked him better.

Now that she had secured a partner, Georgina felt herself relax. She saw that Ann and the Duke were in the first couples with Lord Greystone. Poor Ann! She would not like being so conspicuous. Lord Tansby was introducing Ann to Lord Greystone and his partner, a pretty girl with golden curls. Georgina wondered if it were Miss Stanhope, the blond rage of last season that she had heard so much about.

Ann executed her elegant little curtsy while Greystone bowed. He looked deadly serious and Georgina supposed he must always. He appeared to be what Georgina's old governess would call a 'sourpuss.' Well, she would be interested to know what Ann thought of him.

Lady Tennesby opened the cotillion. As Georgina moved through the changes, she stole glances at Lord Greystone. He was an accomplished dancer, though he did not appear to enjoy himself very much. Lord Tansby was his usual lively self, and Georgina could see he was entertaining Ann with his anecdotes.

Mr. Simons led Georgina through the changes creditably. He was a handsome man, but Georgina knew there was no point in hoping in that direction. Her father would never accept a second son. Georgina thought it was so unfair that second and third sons were the unluckiest of people. Mr. Simons had grown up on an estate, but all that would be his future was to become an officer or clergyman.

After the dance ended, Georgina looked out for Ann. She was speaking with Lord Tansby near the punch bowl. Ann noted Georgina standing alone and made her way over to her.

As Georgina thought to question Ann on her opinion of Lord Greystone, her mother startled her from behind. "I see Ann has met Lord Greystone," Lady Marksley said. "Have you been introduced, Georgina?"

What on earth was her mother doing in the ballroom? She should be safely ensconced at a card table with the dowager. "No," Georgina said. "Not yet."

"We shall fix that," Lady Marksley said with determination.

A sense of impending doom washed over Georgina as she watched her mother make her way over to Lord Tennesby. After a short conversation, Lady Marksley left the ballroom, in search of her card game.

Lord Tennesby approached Lord Greystone. Greystone glanced over at her, and then looked away.

Georgina wished to be swallowed up by the dance floor. To disappear into thin air and never be heard from again.

The man was reluctant to even be introduced! What greater insult to a young lady could there possibly be? None, she knew.

Lord Tennesby said a few more words and Greystone nodded.

Georgina suspected that Lord Greystone had just been told that Lady Marksley and the Dowager were great friends. He'd have to acknowledge her, even though he would clearly rather not.

"Steady on, Georgina," Ann whispered. "He cannot bite you."

Oh but he could, Georgina thought. He could bite her pride, just as he had done in the park. From his manner, it would be obvious to anyone nearby that he did not hold her in any esteem. It would be worse than being Harriet Ledbetter, the loud American that was somehow related to Lord Worthington. Though Miss Ledbetter was invited nearly everywhere, most people studiously avoided her, lest they get trapped into a conversation about how much things cost.

Get a backbone, Georgina. You are not Harriet Ledbetter and you do not discuss the cost of your dress.

Greystone made his way over to her, accompanied by Lord Tennesby.

"May I present Lord Greystone, the Earl of Knightsbridge," Lord Tennesby said. "Lord Greystone, this is Miss Marksley, the daughter of Lord and Lady Marksley."

Georgina curtsied.

Lord Greystone executed a stiff bow. Not particularly deep, Georgina noted.

Lord Tennesby seemed to feel he had done his duty and wandered away.

"I believe you know my cousin," Georgina said, "Miss Carrington."

"We were introduced at the start of the ball," the Earl said.

A long silence ensued. Finally, Ann said, "It is a very pleasant ball."

Georgina nearly laughed despite her embarrassment. That was the sort of thing one said when there was absolutely nothing else to say.

"Quite pleasant," Greystone responded.

Another long silence.

Georgina was determined not to break it. If the great Lord Greystone could not lower himself to make polite conversation, she had no intention of carrying the thing herself.

"I understand you are a horsewoman," the Earl said to Georgina.

Georgina felt anger boiling up in her like a cauldron. She should have expected that. He could not resist alluding to their near collision in Hyde Park. She drew herself up and said, "Of course you understand I am a horsewoman, as your horse and mine came dangerously close this morning. I'll thank you to not refer to the incident again."

Ann clutched her arm. Georgina knew she should stop talking immediately, but she was too angry.

"And by the by, Lord Greystone," she said in as haughty a tone as she could manage, "I was merely riding a horse, not murdering my maid."

Greystone flushed. Georgina felt she finally had the upper hand. And then she felt ridiculous. Why in the world had she mentioned murdering her maid?

Lord Greystone stiffly bowed and stalked off.

"Georgina!" Ann said. "What were you thinking?"

"Nothing sensible," Georgina muttered.

Chapter Three

The ride home from the ball was excruciating. Georgina's mother insisted on knowing the details of her introduction to Lord Greystone. Thank the heavens her mother had not observed it or she would have known it went as poorly as possible. Georgina could only pray her exchange with the Earl had not been overheard by anyone other than Ann.

"Well," Georgina said, trying to put on a bright face for her mother, "he is rather stiff."

Ann looked at Georgina in alarm from her seat on the opposite side of the coach.

Lady Marksley tapped her fan on Georgina's arm. "He is also rather rich," she said. "And good-looking too. He has got a strong jaw and those striking grey-blue eyes. I wonder that you said he was only passable, Georgina. Ann," her mother said, "how did you find Lord Greystone?"

Georgina stared at Ann. This was most problematic. Ann, for all her fine qualities, was a notoriously terrible liar. When Ann was a girl, her governess had questioned her and Edmund about an apple tart that had mysteriously disappeared. Ann had admitted to the crime, and then admitted to every other crime she had committed during her seven short years in the world.

"I found Lord Greystone polite," Ann said. "Though perhaps a bit reserved."

"Humph," her mother said. It was clear to Georgina that she was meant to like Lord Greystone. She suspected her mother of contriving a match with him. It would suit her mother and the dowager to be connected through marriage, however loosely. If she only knew! The very last person she would walk out of the season with was Lord Greystone.

Still, Georgina had to admit, if she had met him under other circumstances, she would have found him handsome. He was tall and broad-shouldered. Her mother was right that he did have a strong jaw. And those eyes…

No matter, Georgina thought. She had not met him under different circumstances. What was done was done. He thought her silly, or fast, or undignified, or something. It grated on her that she did not have his good opinion, even though if she'd had it, she'd have thrown it back in his face. She resolved that, from now on, she would not set one toe out of place. She would be a dignified lady and not do anything, ever again, that would raise an eyebrow. She would be more like Ann. Sweet temperament, always patient, never saying a word out of turn. She would have to consult with Ann on exactly how she managed it.

An hour later, after the house on Berkeley Square was dark and quiet, Georgina took her candle and tiptoed to Ann's room. She poked her head in the door and said, "Are you awake?"

"Yes, Georgina," Ann said. "I thought you might pay me a visit."

Georgina put her candle down on the night table and jumped on Ann's bed. "Did I not tell you he was horrible?" she asked.

Ann sat up and hugged her knees. "But Georgina," she said, "how could you allow yourself to have such an outburst? It was not very lady-like to talk about murdering your maid, whatever made you say it?"

"I hardly know," Georgina admitted. "Earlier in the day I was so aggravated and I kept thinking, well, I was only riding a horse, not murdering my maid." Georgina paused, then she said, "He was so rude that it just came rushing out by itself."

"I cannot imagine what your mother would have said if she had heard you."

"I *can* imagine," Georgina said, "though I'd rather not. Fortunately, she did not hear me. She's quite taken with Lord Greystone, but I am hoping that will pass. I shall pick out some nice young gentleman for her to concentrate on, thereby creating a diversion."

"That would be very wrong, Georgina. You must respect your parents, not try to trick them."

"There," Georgina said. "That is exactly it. You must teach me how to be just like you. You never make a wrong step, Ann, and that's what I intend to do. For the rest of the season I will be beyond reproach. No more galloping, no more outbursts. I will be positively sedate."

Ann giggled.

Georgina crossed her arms. "You laugh? Whatever for? I've just announced a most worthy resolution."

"Truly," Ann said, "you have. I am just trying to picture you as sedate."

"You shall see, Ann. You shall see first thing tomorrow morning."

At dawn, Georgina lay in bed wishing she could jump up and go for a ride. But no, she thought, that would be too ridiculous. It was the first day of the new, beyond reproach, Georgina. She dared not get in the saddle, it would be too difficult to ride Juno and not give the horse her head. She was determined to spend the morning as her mother and Ann did and that meant she had a few long and boring hours ahead of her before it was even time to get out of bed.

Horse's hooves clattered across the cobblestones in the courtyard below. She leapt up and ran to the window. Edmund was on his stallion, Mercury. Poor Edmund, he did not yet know of the new Georgina. He would assume she would be getting ready to go with him for a gallop down Rotten Row.

Georgina thought to throw open the window and tell him all about it. Then she paused. Would Ann throw open the window and shout down to the courtyard? Probably not. She would let her brother knock on the door and then a servant could inform Edmund that nobody in the house was up.

She peered down at Edmund's dark head as he tied off his horse. He was a handsome man, and just as lively as herself. Edmund loved a joke and was popular around town. If Georgina did marry him, she guessed their household would be filled with laughter.

Would laughter be enough?

Georgina supposed it would be better than finding one had married a person like Lord Greystone, whose name might as well be 'Monsieur Morbid.'

As she watched him bang the door knocker, Georgina wondered why Edmund hadn't been at the ball. He had known she would be there. Perhaps he did not think of marrying her after all.

Georgina's musing was interrupted by her maid, Jemma. "Mr. Carrington is downstairs, miss. Shall I get your riding habit?"

"No Jemma," Georgina said. "I shall lay abed until nine and then breakfast with my mother and my cousin Ann."

Jemma peered at her. "Are you ill?"

"Not at all."

"But you're staying in bed?"

"Yes, Jemma. That is what most fashionable young ladies do, so that is what I shall do."

Jemma stared at Georgina, then she said, "I'll tell Mr. Carrington you're ill," and marched from the room.

The time passed slowly, the only entertaining diversion Georgina had was watching Jemma peer around the doorframe every fifteen minutes, shake her head and close the door. It would clearly take some time for Jemma to get accustomed to her new, staying abed, ways. So far, being sedate was tedious, but Georgina had high hopes that the morning would improve once she was actually able to get up and dressed.

The drawing room was quiet. Ann and her mother were engrossed in their embroidery. Georgina pretended to be engrossed in her own, the same piece she had dragged around for the past three years.

Kingston entered with a card on a silver tray. Lady Marksley picked it up. "Ah," she said, "it's Lady Castlereagh. Show her in, Kingston."

Lady Castlereagh? She was the Marchioness of Londonderry, but far more important, she was an Almack's dragon. A fire-breathing Patroness that could incinerate a girl's hopes with the slightest nod. Georgina straightened her gown and ran a hand over her hair. She tucked her embroidery back into the basket, where it spent most of its time anyway.

Lady Castlereagh swept into the room. She was an imposing woman and made Georgina's mother look positively petite. She wore a cream silk dress with a pale blue ribbon, her hair was swept up and framed her face in ringlets.

Georgina and Ann curtsied. Her mother and Lady Castlereagh greeted each other as old friends.

Lady Castlereagh and her mother exchanged pleasantries while Kingston brought in the tea. Georgina sat silent, not daring to make a move that the Lady might disapprove of. She did not even glance over at Ann, though she suspected that Ann was equally frozen.

Kingston bowed out and shut the door while Georgina's mother poured a cup of tea for Lady Castlereagh.

"Now," Lady Castlereagh said, taking her cup, "I can reveal why I've come."

Georgina started. This was not just a social call? She had thought that would be hard enough to get through, but there was more? Had she heard something about the gallop? Or her exchange with Lord Greystone?

As Georgina was imagining having to hand back her voucher, Lady Castlereagh said, "As you know, my dear Lady Marksley, last season was cut unfortunately short due to the fever spreading throughout London."

Georgina remembered that. Her mother and father had returned from London weeks before they were expected, and Ann and Georgina were kept away from them for three days on advice of their local doctor.

"My family physician has informed me," Lady Castlereagh continued, "that there is talk in the medical community that we may well see another fever this year."

"Oh dear," Lady Marksley said. "And poor Georgina's first season, too."

At the mention of her name, Lady Castlereagh turned to Georgina. She could feel the blood creeping into her cheeks under the scrutiny of this formidable lady.

Lady Castlereagh gave her a kind smile. "We will not be so easily defeated, my dear. The Prince of Wales' physician, Sir Henry Halford, and a group of scientific-minded gentleman are attempting to develop a theory on how the fever begins. They believe the conditions in the poor neighborhoods, coupled with finer weather, somehow give birth to the disease. I pointed out that there is no use knowing how the thing begins if you do not know how to stop it. Sir Halford informed me that every gentleman's club in the city has formed a committee. Halford believes that bringing all the best minds in London to the case must surely result in a solution."

Lady Castlereagh drew herself up. "I informed Sir Halford that Almack's *would not* be left out of this noble cause. The Patronesses of Almack's feel it is their duty to help save the season. We are quite determined and are arranging our committee at this very moment. We invite Miss Marksley and Miss Carrington to attend."

"My dear Lady Castlereagh," Georgina's mother said, "you would not propose that the girls venture into these low neighborhoods to look for a cause of fever?"

"Certainly not. We will have soldiers for that. No, the committees are for planning. Just what is really causing these fevers and what can be done about it? That's what we've got to determine. As I told Sir Halford, it's all well and good to talk about noxious vapors being the culprit, but where are they coming from and how can we rid ourselves of them?"

"In that case," Georgina's mother said, "the girls would be honored."

"Yes, ma'am," Georgina and Ann said in unison.

Lady Castlereagh tapped her fan on the side of her chair and said, "Today at two."

Chapter Four

After Lady Castlereagh left, Georgina thought about all she had said. A fever cutting the season short would be disappointing, but nothing compared to seeing her parents or Ann fall ill. And what about all those poor neighborhoods? They were always the hardest hit. The ton could take to their carriages and flee to the country, but the poor must stay just where they were.

Georgina blushed when she realized that she had never given the people who lived in such places a thought. Who were they? What did they do all day? What did they think about? What did they dream about? Certainly they wished their children safe, and what a misery it must be to see the fever take over a household. She knew from visiting farmers on her family's estate that there were people who lived in one room together. Her father was kinder than most and would add rooms to a tenancy that had a growing family, but it was still little enough. She suspected the life of the poor in London must be a thousand times worse.

It suddenly occurred to Georgina to notice something that had always been right under her nose on the estate. The tenancies were at different elevations and the lower elevations always seemed to experience the most sickness and disease. She had assumed that was because the richer tenancies happened to be at the higher elevations. But what if it were something in the elevation itself? Perhaps noxious vapors tended to drift down, rather than up?

She was determined to do her best on the committee. Still, the entire idea seemed odd to Georgina. It did seem like a subject best left to the gentleman's clubs. She wondered if this were some scheme by the Patronesses to get a closer look at the girls they had invited to Almack's. The thought sent a shiver of terror to her heart. If that were so, and a girl was found to be wanting in some way, what then?

Georgina cheered herself by remembering that she had already decided to be sedate and had begun that very morning. So far, she had not stuck one toe out of place.

Georgina realized her mother was speaking while she had drifted off into her own thoughts.

"Of course," her mother said, "this is all quite unusual. However, it is also a unique opportunity. Gain the approval of the Patronesses and no door will ever be closed to you."

Georgina sighed. "And I suppose the opposite is equally true," she said. "Gain the disapproval of the Patronesses and doors will slam from here to Scotland."

"That is true, my dear," her mother said. "So have a care."

Georgina had thought her new attempt at sedate would result in an endlessly boring day. Now, having the two o'clock appointment at Almack's looming ahead of her, she felt the time rushing by unaccountably fast. She was filled with dread at the prospect of being under such close scrutiny of the Patronesses. The balls were easy enough to manage – simply arrive before eleven, dressed appropriately, sip lemonade and dance. Georgina had made it a practice to keep her distance from the Patronesses, lest she say or do something they would not approve of. She felt they would like her better if they did not know her so well.

But why did she think that of herself? Was she really so terrible? No, certainly not. Though she recognized that she could be impulsive in both word and deed. Edmund usually did not help the case, as he was just the same. She had thought that wonderful until now. Now though, she began to wonder if marriage to someone so similar in temperament might not lead to difficulties. Who would be there to rein them both in?

If she did marry Edmund, she'd have to convince Ann to come live with them forever so that there would be someone there to hold up a hand and say, "You are about to go too far."

Georgina smiled at the idea of Ann as she and Edmund's governess. No, Ann would make her own life and would not be there to act as nanny. If she were to have a life with Edmund, they would both need to learn to control themselves. That brought Georgina's mind back to the old question – did she *want* a life with Edmund?

Jemma handed Georgina her gloves. Ann poked her head around the door. "Are you ready, Georgina? We must not be late."

As the carriage made its way to King Street, Georgina fumbled with her fan and pulled at her gloves and rearranged herself on her seat.

"Georgina," Ann said. "You are as fidgety as a cat."

"And so would you be if you were me," Georgina said.

"Whatever do you mean?" Ann asked.

"You know perfectly well what I mean, Ann. Look at you! You are the picture of calm and reserve. You would not say anything that the Patronesses would disapprove of in the next hundred years. But I? I am terrified I shall do or say something I may regret."

Ann squeezed Georgina's hand. "You are being entirely too hard on yourself. Lord Greystone has shaken your confidence. Yes, you can sometimes be a bit too high-spirited. But you are also a perfectly charming, almost annoyingly pretty, young lady of good breeding and excellent manners. You have been given a voucher to Almack's, every hostess in London is glad to see you and now, you have been specially invited by Lady Castlereagh to join this important committee. Chin up, Georgina."

Georgina felt a bit better after Ann's speech. She patted Ann's hand. "I shall follow you, dear Ann, and do just as you do. I know I shall never go wrong doing that."

The carriage had turned down King Street and Almack's loomed ahead. It was not a particularly prepossessing building, being of white stone and plain proportions. Yet, it held a power over the young ladies of the season that could not be understated. A girl who failed at Almack's was a girl who had simply failed.

Georgina smiled to herself as she remembered her imaginings of this bastion of good taste. The year before, as she languished in the country and dreamed of coming out, she had imagined herself boldly taking Almack's by storm. She had known there were Patronesses, but back then they had existed far in the background as a group of kindly old ladies who would conveniently make introductions. She had understood the reality of it at her first ball. The Patronesses were awesome to behold.

"Never fear, Georgina," Ann said. "You will not be the subject of discussion come Monday night."

"Monday night?" Georgina said. "What is happening on Monday night?"

"The Patronesses meet every Monday night to discuss who should be invited and who should be banned."

Georgina had known nothing about the Monday night meetings. She felt slightly faint getting out of the carriage.

Georgina and Ann were shown to a supper room. Eight other girls, most of whom Georgina knew, were already seated. The

Honorable Miss Smith, a tall girl with auburn hair that Georgina had often seen riding a magnificent chestnut through Hyde Park. Miss Cavendish and her cousin Miss Templeton, both reserved to the point of being nearly speechless. Miss Hargrave, who had a reputation for being bold, though she seemed to keep that quality quite under wraps when the Patronesses were nearby. Miss Hastings-Bass, who Georgina had heard was on her third season with nervous parents in tow. Miss Lennox, who Georgina and Ann liked immensely, despite her tendency to be bookish. And finally, the girl with the blond curls that Georgina had observed Lord Greystone dancing with at the Tennesby's ball. Georgina discovered quickly enough that her guess on the evening had been correct as she heard her addressed as Miss Stanhope.

Georgina and Ann sat in the empty seats at the low end of the table.

Lady Castlereagh sat at the head of the table. She stood and the girls fell silent. "As we are all here," she said, "we shall begin. First, I will tell you that the other Patronesses and I thought very carefully on who to include on this important committee. Consider it an honor that you have been selected and I have no doubt that when word goes round about it I will be inundated with visits from disappointed mothers.

"That said," Lady Castlereagh continued, "propriety is our utmost concern. You will be chaperoned at all times by myself or Lady Worthington, however, you may find that we hold discussions that veer toward the vulgar. That cannot be helped, as we are proposing to discuss the lower neighborhoods of the city. Not the usual conversation for young ladies, but we feel we have a group of girls here who will someday be leaders in society and so there are times that realities, no matter how unpleasant, must be faced.

"Our first challenge," Lady Castlereagh said, "is to properly understand the problem. The Prince of Wales's physician, Sir Halford, along with Lord Greystone, the Earl of Knightsbridge, have kindly agreed to outline their findings."

Lord Greystone? Why? Why Lord Greystone? Was there nowhere safe from that man? What has he got to do with fevers?

Georgina was in Almack's, under the direct gaze of Lady Castlereagh, about to be faced with the one man who could undo all her plans to be sedate.

Well, he would not do it. No matter what he said or how rude he was, she was determined not to respond in kind.

But, oh! The last thing she'd said to him. That ridiculous statement about not murdering her maid. It would take everything she had to ignore the condescension she was sure she would be faced with.

Ann squeezed her hand under the table. She squeezed back until she noticed Ann wince.

Lord Greystone entered the room, followed by Sir Halford.

Georgina was not surprised to see that Lord Greystone wore his usual grim expression. Sir Halford was an unremarkable-looking man, shorter than Greystone, but Georgina noticed he had keen, intelligent eyes.

The men bowed and Lord Greystone glanced around the room. He nodded to Miss Stanhope. Georgina thought there must be something between them and would not be surprised to hear of an engagement. Miss Stanhope, for all her pretty blond curls, looked as humorless as Greystone.

His eyes traveled around the room until his gaze settled on Georgina. He stared at her.

Georgina felt defiance welling up in her breast. She had been in the regular habit of giving in to her feelings and until just yesterday she would have made some saucy remark. But no more. From now on, he would not be able to pry the slightest disagreeable feeling from her. She smiled and slightly nodded her head to acknowledge his notice.

Lord Greystone looked away. As Georgina relaxed, she noticed Miss Stanhope was staring at her. Poor girl! She had no doubt completely misread Greystone's attention.

Lady Castlereagh made the introductions around the room, then she said, "Gentleman, thank you for coming to speak to our little committee. We poor females will do our best to help this noble cause. Rest assured, Almack's stands firmly behind you in your efforts. Now, if you would be so good as to explain to the ladies what your current theories are."

Sir Halford bowed and said, "Thank you, Lady Castlereagh. Ladies," he said, addressing the table, "far be it for me to dismiss assistance coming from any quarter. Further, it is my experience that while it is true that only men are suited to be physicians, the female is not without skill. Ladies tend to be observant of the human condition, and you may well find you have something to offer in these discussions."

Sir Halford adjusted his cravat and said sternly, "What will not be helpful is if you choose to carry on like a gaggle of simpering females."

Simpering females? Georgina hadn't seen one simper yet.

"Lady Castlereagh assured me," Sir Halford continued, "that you were all chosen for your sharp minds and sensible dispositions. There will be no false swooning on this committee! No fan waving, no tears, no hysterics! If you are not willing to deal with the realities of London, get back in your carriage and go home!"

Georgina saw Lord Greystone hide a smile. It was the first smile she had seen from him. She was trying not to smile herself – Sir Halford seemed determined to turn them all into soldiers.

Lady Castlereagh laid a hand on the doctor's arm. "Very good, Sir Halford. I think we understand you perfectly. There were any number of girls I might have invited that would have swooned and fanned you right out of the room, but I did not invite them. Never fear, sir, here you will only find sensible modesty."

Georgina wondered what exactly sensible modesty looked like. As Lady Castlereagh seemed to approve of it, she would have to get Ann's opinion on it later.

"Very Good," Sir Halford said, looking much relieved that he would not be faced with fan-waving, swooning females. "First, Lord Greystone will show you a map of where the fever took hold last year."

Lord Greystone rolled a sheet of vellum over the table. Georgina leaned forward in her chair to get a better view. Whole areas of London were blacked out; other areas were shaded grey.

"As you can see," Lord Greystone said, "the poor neighborhoods were hardest hit. Whitechapel, Shoreditch, Bethnal Green, Devil's Acre, Clerkenwell, Spitalfields and the list goes on. The poorer the neighborhood, the harder it was hit. It is always so."

"We believe the cause is noxious vapors." Sir Halford said. He paused and glared around the room in case any girl thought to swoon at the mention of noxious vapors. Georgina smiled. So far, everyone had remained perfectly upright in their chair.

Satisfied that there would be no female to scrape off the floor, Sir Halford continued. "There are any number of theories on it. We know the fine weather sets it off, so perhaps heat creates the vapors. We know that there are many unsavory types living in these neighborhoods, thieves and their lot." Sir Halford once again paused and peered at the girls. No one had swooned at the mention of thieves. "Very good," Sir Halford said. "So as these unsavory types have low morals, perhaps this is some sort of divine retribution. Though I, personally, do not believe that particular theory. The point is, nothing has been proven and we have never discovered a method of driving back the fever. Once it arrives, it runs its course as we stand helplessly by. That is what we're about with these committees."

Georgina could only think back to Marksley Manor and what she had observed there. The slovenlier tenants at the bottom of the hill tended to get ill more often. Somehow, the noxious vapors were gathering around them, and not the tenants at the top of the hill.

"I've done as you asked, Lady Castlereagh," Sir Halford said. "Send either myself or Lord Greystone a note if you believe you have something of relevance emerging from your committee."

Lord Greystone bowed and swept up his map. Georgina observed he and Sir Halford carefully. She did not believe that either of them thought that they would hear from this particular committee again. She blushed. It was clear to her, if not to Lady Castlereagh, that the two men were merely humoring Lady Castlereagh's whim and did not think females could possibly contribute to the cause.

After the men had left the room and the door had been shut, Lady Castlereagh stood and said, "As you can see, we have a challenge ahead. Those men do not believe we will uncover anything of value. But," she said, drawing to her full height, "we are Almack's. If anyone is to save the season, it had best be us. I am determined that we shall save the day. Now, we shall go around the room and each girl can express her thoughts on the matter. Miss Stanhope?"

Georgina noticed that most of the girls look terrified. No one, including herself, had thought they would do any speaking. The only girl who looked as composed as a portrait was her dear Ann.

"Well, Lady Castlereagh," Miss Stanhope stuttered. "If it be noxious vapors that cause the distress, then perhaps what's needed is wind to blow it away?"

Georgina bit her lip.

"Yes, that might well help," Lady Castlereagh said, "but the question is, where would we get the wind? You see, what we are looking for here is something we can do."

Miss Stanhope nodded and looked as if she might cry.

"Now my girl," Lady Castlereagh said kindly, "do not be distressed. This is not a dinner party where you have said something gauche. This is a working committee and we will go through very many wrong ideas until we get to something right."

Miss Stanhope and the rest of the girls seemed to take heart from that statement. Lady Castlereagh went around the room, gathering the girl's thoughts. Some of them were quite novel, such as setting blocks of ice on every street corner to cool the air.

Georgina half-listened as she reviewed what she knew of life at the manor. It was clearly something about the elevation of the houses that caused more illness at the bottom of the hill and less at the top. And just as in the city, fevers were more likely during warm weather than cold.

She pictured the tenancies in her imagination. A sudden remembrance leapt into her mind. Just the year before, she had visited a tenant at the top of the hill. The tenant's wife was suffering from rheumatism and Georgina had brought her some tea and sugar. It had been a warm, still morning and the smell of the outhouse had filled the air. Georgina had noticed tiny rivulets emerging from underneath its walls and running down the hill. She had quickly covered her nose with her handkerchief and thought that must be highly unpleasant for the tenant at the bottom of the hill. Perhaps that was it. Perhaps being exposed to an overflowing outhouse was why the lower elevations suffered so badly.

Lady Castlereagh had come to Ann. "Lady Castlereagh," Ann said in her serenely calm voice, "I've not much to add, except something I have always noted in my father's cows. When disease strikes the herd, those that were strongest to begin are most likely to survive. They are strong because they eat well and grow fat. This makes me wonder if these poor neighborhoods are more vulnerable to fever because they do not have enough food."

"You could well be right, Miss Carrington, but I do not see how we could feed all of London. Miss Marksley?"

Georgina felt all eyes upon her. She supposed her theory would be dismissed, but she took heart that she would be no worse off than the other girls. The only girl who had received a truly disapproving look from Lady Castlereagh was Miss Clandsbridge, who had only said, "I'm sure I don't know, Lady Castlereagh." Georgina did not think Miss Clandsbridge would be returning for another meeting. The important thing was not to be right, the important thing was just to have an idea.

Georgina took a deep breath. "Lady Castlereagh," she said, "as my cousin Ann noted, I can only say what I've observed on my father's estate. His estate is comprised of rolling hills. I have noticed, from year to year, that the tenants at the higher elevations are less likely to suffer fevers in the warm weather and the tenants in the low-lying areas are always the hardest hit. I think I may know why, but I am not sure how to say it, as it is a delicate…." Georgina trailed off. She really was not sure how to describe the outhouse problem to a group of gentlewoman, one of which was the proper Lady Castlereagh.

"Out with it, Miss Marksley," Lady Castlereagh said. "We have no room for false modesty here."

Georgina thought she had better just say it as directly as she could. "Yes, of course, Lady Castlereagh," she said. "The problem may have to do with the…outhouses. Last year, I noticed that an outhouse at the top of the hill was…overflowing. It was making its way down the hill. The tenant family below was indeed struck with a fever soon after my observation. I suspect the noxious vapors may be coming from…the outhouse. If that is so, then the underlying cause of the fevers may be lack of proper drainage."

There. She had said it and Lady Castlereagh did not appear shocked. Some of the other girls initially seemed shocked, but when they noted that Lady Castlereagh did not, they quickly gave it up.

"Drainage?" Lady Castlereagh said. "Sir Halford mentioned the stench of these neighborhoods. No doubt the drainage is appalling. The question is, what could we do about it?"

"Lady Castlereagh?" Georgina said. "If I may?"

"Yes, of course Miss Marksley. Proceed."

"You mentioned to my mother that soldiers were ready to assist in any endeavor the committee might devise."

"I did," Lady Castlereagh said. "The Prince of Wales wants to save the season as much as anybody and is happy to oblige."

At the mention of the Prince of Wales, Georgina blushed. Everyone knew he was a wild rake; her mother had told her to steer well clear of him. "Yes," Georgina said, "so might not the soldiers go from street to street, assessing the drainage and devising a plan to improve it?"

Lady Castlereagh was silent for a moment. Then she said, "Yes, that might be just the thing. It certainly is worth attempting. Ladies, I shall send Lord Greystone a note this very day and let he and Sir Halford know that the Almack's committee requests his presence. We will convene a meeting and, Miss Marksley, you will provide the description of our plan."

Chapter Five

Lady Castlereagh left the girls under the watchful eye of Lady Worthington. Tea was served, and Georgina distractedly nibbled on a biscuit. Some day in the not too distant future she would have to discuss outhouses in front of Lord Greystone. She'd have been better off following Miss Clandsbridge's lead and just said, 'I'm sure I don't know.'

"What a wonderful idea, Georgina," Ann said.

"Was it?" Georgina asked. "I hadn't quite envisioned having to explain it to Sir Halford and Lord Grey-Tone."

"Georgina!" Ann scolded. "Do not call him that!"

"I am sorry, I meant to say Lord Gloomy."

"Georgina," Ann said in a tone that conveyed her disapproval.

"Ah, see?" Georgina said. "When I am not concentrating at my very best, I slip right back into my old ways. It shall take a lot of effort to be like you, Ann."

"Nonsense," Ann said. "You are lovely as you are, just have a care. There are other ears about just now."

As Ann had noted, there *were* other ears about just now. She must focus on being sedate. Miss Stanhope approached. After exchanging pleasantries, Miss Stanhope said, "I see you are acquainted with Lord Greystone."

"Yes, indeed," Georgina said. "And yourself?"

"Why yes," Miss Stanhope stuttered. "We were introduced last season."

Georgina had no doubt that the blond Miss Stanhope had set her cap on Lord Greystone. If she were not in the midst of practicing being sedate, Georgina would put the girl out of her misery and tell her there was not, and never would be, anything between her and the Earl of serious.

"We were both introduced at Lady Tennesby's ball," Ann helpfully put in. "Miss Marksley's mother is a great friend of the dowager."

Poor Miss Stanhope. Georgina knew Ann had pointed out the connection to put Miss Stanhope at her ease, but Georgina thought she had done quite the opposite. Miss Stanhope was probably imagining that Georgina's mother and the dowager had a scheme to marry them off.

"Your idea about the…you know," Miss Stanhope said, "it was very clever. Though I would be a frightful wreck if I were the one to present it to Lord Greystone and Sir Halford."

"Fear not, Miss Stanhope," Georgina said. "It will be I that is the frightful wreck." She said it in jest, though in truth she had no doubt she would be.

Georgina's mother paused, the teapot hung in the air. "You spoke to Lady Castlereagh about outhouses?"

"It does sound shocking," Georgina said, "but in truth, Lady Castlereagh quite approved. We will request soldiers to look into the matter."

"I cannot say I understand much of how these committees work, but I suppose if you've gained Lady Castlereagh's approval than you have represented yourself quite creditably, my dear."

Ann said, "Our Georgina will be explaining the whole scheme to Lord Greystone and Sir Halford."

Georgina's mother looked at her with interest. Georgina wished Ann hadn't mentioned Lord Greystone, her mother quite approved of the Earl.

"Yes," Georgina said, "I am rather quaking about it."

"Whatever for, Georgi?" her mother said. "You are quite well-spoken."

"That may be," Georgina said, "but I have had no experience discussing outhouses in front of gentleman."

The days passed in a sort of dream-like state for Georgina. Not even a visit to Vauxhall or shopping on Bond Street could entirely capture her attention. Each time she arrived home to Berkeley Square, she looked for the dreaded note from Lady Castlereagh.

On the third day of waiting it arrived. "Dear Miss Marksley and Miss Carrington, your presence is requested to attend the committee at Almack's on Wednesday at two o'clock. Warmest, Lady Castlereagh."

That was tomorrow.

Georgina had fought her nerves all the way to King Street while Ann had reassured her. Ann finally gave up and said, "Take heart, Georgina, whatever is to be today, at least by this evening it will be over."

That had been the first thing Ann had said that actually did cheer Georgina up. Ann was exactly right. She was not facing an eternity of discomfort, just one afternoon. By supper it would be entirely over. Whether or not her theory was correct, she had done her best and no one could fault her for it.

Georgina entered the supper room and noted that Lord Greystone and Sir Halford were already in attendance. Both men looked slightly bored. She was sure they believed they were about to hear something entirely nonsensical and had merely agreed to come as a courtesy to Lady Castlereagh. After all, Greystone would not dare insult a Patroness. To do so would mean losing the right to attend the Almack's balls and his reputation would suffer as a result. Sir Halford no doubt felt powerless to refuse the summons.

Miss Stanhope and the rest of the girls had taken their usual places. Miss Clandsbridge's chair was empty and Georgina had no doubt it would remain so. For all her trepidation about explaining her idea, Georgina supposed it would have been far worse to explain to her mother that she had been dismissed from the committee for the lack of one.

Lady Worthington kept a sharp eye on the girls, though Georgina had no idea what sort of impropriety she was on the look-out for. Lady Castlereagh swept into the room.

"Gentleman, thank you for coming," she said. "We would not dream of wasting your valuable time and you were already introduced at the last committee meeting so we shall proceed directly. Miss Marksley?"

Georgina saw all eyes turn to her. She must speak so soon? She had thought there would be more talk before she was yielded the floor. Never mind, Georgina, chin up and get on with it.

"Yes," Georgina said. "Thank you. As Lady Castlereagh mentioned, we do not want to waste your time, gentleman, so I will be as concise as I am able. I will also be as direct as I am able, though the subject matter is…a bit shocking."

Sir Halford pointed at her. "No swooning, Miss."

Georgina smiled. She should have known Sir Halford would relieve the tension. She felt herself relax. "I would not dream of it, Sir Halford," she said.

As Georgina explained her theory that the overflowing outhouse of her father's tenant caused the fever of the tenants below, she noticed Lord Greystone appeared actually interested in what she was saying. Sir Halford stood with his arms folded, appearing to take what she said seriously, also. Georgina gained confidence. Even if they discounted her theory all together, they clearly did not think it was foolish. She ended by saying, "So we were wondering if the soldiers might not go from street to street in these neighborhoods and assess the drainage and do something about it."

"Now that's the first sensible idea I've heard come out of these blasted committees, eh Greystone?" Sir Halford said.

Lord Greystone nodded.

"Certainly better than Lord Gamesly's idea that we employ the clergy to pray away the fevers," Sir Halford said.

Georgina bit her lip to stop a smile. Everyone knew Lord Gamesly to be overly pious. His daughter was out, but she might well not have been considering how few entertainments she was allowed.

"The question is, gentleman, will you direct the soldiers to act upon Miss Marksley's suggestion?" Lady Castlereagh asked.

"We could," Lord Greystone said. "I have been to some of these neighborhoods with Sir Halford, looking for clues as to what causes the fever. The outhouses are remarkably few and most...waste...is deposited directly on the street."

At the mention of waste, Georgina saw some of the girls might actually swoon, despite Sir Halford's determination that they should not.

"If the theory is correct," Lord Greystone continued, "then it would account for why the fever is always so much more rampant in the city than it is in the country."

"And it would account for why it comes with the warm weather," Sir Halford said. "As of course when the temperature rises--"

"That may be more detail than we require," Lady Castlereagh said, cutting him off. "These are intelligent, sensible girls, but one may still go too far in testing their fortitude."

"Quite right," Sir Halford said. "Well," he said, straightening his cravat, "I am encouraged. We've finally got something to try."

Lord Greystone bowed and said, "Congratulations, Miss Marksley."

Georgina felt unaccountably pleased. There was something gratifying in having Monsieur Morbid acknowledge her idea.

Plans were made to deploy soldiers around the poorer neighborhoods. They would assess the conditions and make suitable arrangements to improve the conditions. Now, all there was to do was wait. Had Georgina saved the season, and saved lives in the process? Or had she sent his majesty's force on a fool's errand? Only time would tell.

Chapter Six

The Almack's committee continued to meet every Wednesday. Lord Greystone and Sir Halford did not attend, but they sent regular updates to Lady Castlereagh. She had plastered a map of London onto a canvas and it sat on an artist's easel near the top of the table. At each meeting, Lady Castlereagh read the note from Sir Halford detailing where the soldiers had been. Georgina was tasked with shading out the streets and neighborhoods where improvements had been made. They had made good progress.

News of the fever committees had spread throughout the ton. Georgina was recognized as having made some sort of contribution, though no one knew quite what, since it would be entirely too inelegant to discuss outhouses and drainage at a ball. It was just said that she was a clever girl, and left at that.

The only thing Georgina truly fretted about was Edmund. Something was happening to him and she was not sure what it was. First, he had stopped appearing in all the usual places. She expected to see him at a ball or a rout, and then he did not appear and gave her some flimsy excuse. Then the excuses had ended because he had stopped calling at Berkeley Square. She suspected he was off carousing with some of his wilder friends, and this gave her pause when she thought of the idea of marriage. Would he be so then? Would she always wonder where he was?

Then came the news that Edmund's father had arrived in town. That, in itself, was odd enough. Everybody knew that Sir Carrington hated town. Odder than that, though, is that it had been a secret. As Georgina entered the drawing room one morning, she overheard her mother say, "Tell Sir Carrington I will attend him this afternoon." When she had offered to go on the call, her mother had refused and directed Georgina to speak no further about it.

Georgina caught Ann in the hall and steered her to the library. The room was vast and filled floor to ceiling with books. Georgina's father did not gamble or hunt. The two luxuries he allowed himself were his club, where he ate nearly every meal when he was in town, and collecting books.

They settled into a cozy corner that her father had set up especially for Georgina, hoping to encourage her to love books as much as he.

"Whatever is the matter, Georgina?" Ann asked.

"Your father is in town," Georgina said. She had been about to ask Ann if she had known it, but she saw clearly enough that she had not.

"My father? Are you certain? My father never comes to town. I just had a letter from him a week ago, he said nothing of it."

"I doubt I am supposed to tell you. I heard of it quite by chance and my mother did not want to speak about it. I think it must have something to do with Edmund," Georgina said.

"Why do you think so?"

"Have you not noticed, Ann, that everywhere we expect him to be, he is not? He has not attended any of the Almack's balls recently, he was not at the Stonebridge's rout which was unaccountable considering how closely your families are connected and when was the last time he called here?"

Ann looked thoughtful. "I did, indeed, notice his absence at the Stonebridge's. I was really vexed that he would be so rude. I had intended to speak with him about it and sent him a note to attend me, but he has not yet answered it."

"I am afraid he has fallen in with a bad crowd and somehow gotten himself into some trouble," Georgina said.

"Perhaps," Ann said. "Though I fear he may be ill. It is so unlike Edmund to disappear." Ann smiled. "If he were to absent himself every time he got himself into a scrape we should never see him."

Edmund ill? Georgina had not even considered that possibility. She was ashamed of herself for thinking the worst without considering what else might be the matter. Dear Edmund! What if he were facing some grave disease and his father had arrived to supervise his care?

"We must find out, Ann. I do not know why it should be a secret from us."

"I do not understand either" Ann said, "but if your mother has asked you not to speak about it and my father has deemed not to tell me he is in town, then I must trust they have good reason. We must just be patient, Georgina, and see what comes of this visit. We will be told something when we are meant to know it."

Georgina stared at the wall of books in front of her. She knew she should follow Ann's advice. She was certain Ann's judgment was correct, since it invariably was. Still, she could not just be patient. Somehow, she had to discover the truth of what was happening to Edmund. If he were ill, she would go to him and be his nurse. She would wheedle the information out of her mother somehow. It would just take the right moment to broach the subject.

The Duke of Bedford's ball was one of the most talked-about of the season. If Edmund were out anywhere, Georgina thought, he would surely be there. Edmund had a great admiration for Lord Bedford's knowledge of horseflesh and had been eager to make his acquaintance.

Georgina had worn one of her best gowns, a lovely dark blue satin. She knew that pale colors were all the fashion, but the bolder color suited her dark hair and matched her eyes. She gazed around the ball room.

"I do not see him," Georgina whispered to Ann.

"Nor I," Ann replied.

"I think," Georgina said, "that if he does not attend Lord Bedford's ball, we can be sure Edmund must really be ill."

"Oh my," Ann said.

"I know," Georgina said, patting Ann's arm, "it is a frightening thought."

"That is not what I refer to, Georgina. Lord Greystone is on the other side of the ball room and he is staring at you. He has been for more than a minute."

"Lord Glum? Whatever for?" Georgina asked. She said it lightly, intending to be amusing, but her insides were quaking. Had something gone wrong with her plan to avert the fever? It seemed the only possible answer. Lord Greystone, as far as she knew him, did not flirt. And were he to flirt, she would be the last person he would turn his attention to. No, somehow, she had made a mistake and he was letting her know it.

"And now he is coming this way," Ann said, using her fan to hide a smile.

"Do not tease, Ann! Perhaps he has been staring at someone behind me," Georgina said hopefully. She glanced over her shoulder, wishing to see Miss Stanhope. There was no one behind her but a group of old men arranging to play cards.

"I do not tease," Ann said. "He looks quite determined."

Georgina stole a glance. Greystone did look quite determined. Lord Berthsley attempted to engage him in conversation, but found himself talking to the air. Well, if she were about to be scolded, she would not succumb easily. It was one thing to be sedate, and quite another to be one of Lord Gloomy's victims. She would not stand for it.

Lord Greystone stood in front of her and bowed. "Miss Marksley and Miss Carrington," he said.

Georgina and Ann curtsied. "Lord Greystone," Georgina said.

Greystone looked over Georgina's head and said, "We believe we are seeing success with your scheme. There have been no reports of fever, though a fortnight of fine weather has gone by."

That was unexpected. It was the first compliment the man had ever paid her. Though she noticed he avoided looking at her as he said it. She supposed it pained him, but he felt he must say it as a gentleman.

"I pray our good luck continues," Georgina said.

"My cousin is too modest," Ann said.

"Yes," Greystone said quietly.

A long and awkward silence ensued. Georgina willed Ann to say something vague about the ballroom, but Ann stood silently by, smiling.

"Miss Marksley," Lord Greystone said. "May I have the first dance?"

What? Why did he want to dance with her? He should be dancing with Miss Stanhope. Georgina wished she could make him unsay it, it would be the most uncomfortable dance of her life. Whatever would they talk about? Still, she knew that to refuse him meant she'd have to sit out the entire ball.

"Yes," she said, feeling as if her voice came from somewhere outside the room.

Lord Greystone bowed and stalked off.

"What in the world was that?" Georgina asked.

"I think he likes you, Georgina," Ann said.

"Do not be ridiculous. Lord Somber finds me odious. No, he means to punish me in some way. You saw how he could not even look at me. And what will Miss Stanhope think? He should be dancing with her!"

"Well," Ann said, laughing, "regardless of what he should be doing, what he will be doing is dancing with you."

As much as Georgina wished to delay it, the first dance approached ever nearer. She heard the musicians tuning and wished they would all be taken ill and have to go home. She wished Miss Stanhope would appear and Greystone would suddenly remember how much he liked her and somehow make his excuses to Georgina. She even thought of asking her mother to demand her presence at the card table. Ann found the situation amusing.

"It's only a dance, Georgina. He will not bite. In any case, I think you may have misjudged him."

"Misjudged him? However so?"

"You think him serious to the point of rudeness, but perhaps that is because his nature is so different from Edmund's. You are used to my brother's free and easy ways and Lord Greystone is more thoughtful. Frankly, where my brother is boyish, Greystone is a man."

Georgina looked at Ann with raised eyebrows. "This is new," she said. "Since when did you become enamored with Lord Greystone?" As she said it, she thought of Ann's comment. Was there anything in it? It was true that she and the Earl had met under unfortunate circumstances and disliked each other immediately. But then it was also true that he had found merit in her scheme to avert the fever. Had she thought badly of him simply because he was so different from Edmund?

And what of Edmund? He had still not made an appearance. She had dearly hoped to see him at the ball to assure herself that he was well. She had not found an opportune time to question her mother further, but if she did not see Edmund this evening, she was determined to confront her on the morrow.

"Miss Marksley."

Lord Greystone stood before her. The dreaded moment had arrived. She curtsied and allowed herself to be led to the dance floor.

The musicians struck up a cotillion. The problem with the cotillion, Georgina thought, was there was entirely too much time to talk.

Greystone took her hand. She could feel the warmth of it through her glove and it felt strong and yet, surprisingly gentle.

As they moved through the dance, Georgina wracked her mind for something to say. She was accustomed to dancing with gay young men who would amuse her with anecdotes and flirt mercilessly. She could expect no such thing from Greystone. He met her eyes with a thoughtful expression. Good Lord, what did he mean by it?

The other couples around them talked and laughed as they went through the changes. She and Lord Greystone must appear the most ridiculous couple to ever have danced in London. She was certain it was noted by onlookers.

"Lord Greystone, how come you to be of a scientific turn of mind," she said, thinking of his involvement with Sir Halford and hoping to land on a subject he found interesting.

"Ah," he said. "You presume I must be interested in scientific discoveries due to my connection with Sir Halford."

The man was infuriating. Of course that was what she had thought. What else would she have thought?

"Yes," Georgina said. "I did presume that."

"I am less interested in science and more interested in the welfare of people," he said. "My involvement with Sir Halford sprang from my concern over how these epidemics we experience every year are affecting the lower classes."

Georgina felt as if she had been slapped. Now she saw his whole scheme. While she had been blithely going along, pleased that she may have had some hand in saving the season, he had been waiting to point out her selfishness. Georgina colored. He was right. Her first care should have been the welfare of the people of London, not the welfare of balls and dinner parties. Still, just because he was right did not mean he was right to throw it in her face.

She suddenly realized that Lord Greystone had been speaking while she had been seething. "I'm sorry, what?" she said, distractedly.

"I understand you are to be congratulated," Greystone said, looking more serious than ever.

Oh, this was rich, Georgina thought. Not satisfied with hurling one insult her way, now he would point out how silly it was that she had been recognized throughout the ton as having some involvement in the fever committees.

"Lord Greystone," she said in a low tone, "I was asked by Lady Castlereagh to sit on the committee and so I did. I have not asked anyone to applaud my efforts. I do not see where the crime is."

Lord Greystone looked confused. "Lady Castlereagh?" he asked. "I was speaking of your engagement."

Georgina stopped short. "What engagement?"

"I thought, well I thought I had heard," Greystone stuttered, "that you were engaged to your cousin. Edmund Carrington."

"I am not!" Georgina said.

The rest of the dance passed in silence between them. Georgina could not have carried on any further conversation with the man if her life depended on it. What in the world did he mean by it? First, he insults her. Then he announces she is engaged to Edmund. And now he is going through his paces with a smile on his face, as if nothing had happened.

Georgina paused. He was smiling. Lord Gloom appeared to be amused. So, she supposed, his only humor was in another's distress.

That fits. He must like nothing better than having the upper hand. Well, he had done it and she hoped he was satisfied and that was the last she would see of him.

The dance finally ended. Lord Greystone bowed and offered to get her a glass of punch. Georgina stammered something about needing to find Ann and hurried off.

The rest of the ball passed by in a blur. Georgina danced most dances, but made a terrible partner. She was distracted and not at all her usual lively self. As she reflected on the dance with Greystone, she could not make heads or tails of it. Why would he go to such lengths to insult her? Why not just avoid her? And where in the world had he heard she was engaged to Edmund? Had other people heard the rumor? It did not appear so, most of the gentleman of her acquaintance were as flirtatious as ever.

It occurred to Georgina that it may well have been one of Edmund's jokes. He was always saying something he really should not have, just for amusement's sake. Greystone would be unlikely to see the joke, as he was not a particularly joking individual. Georgina remembered that Edmund had mentioned that Greystone belonged to his club. Perhaps that was where the exchange took place. And yet, on that awful day in Hyde Park they had seemed so cold to one another that it did not seem likely that they would engage in any sort of conversation.

She would be angry with Edmund if she found that he had used her as part of a jest. On the other hand, if he had, then he was not laying abed ill.

The next morning, Georgina rose early and lay in wait in the breakfast room for her mother. She had told Ann of the scheme and Ann had very much disapproved, but had agreed to delay her arrival.

Georgina stood at the side table, filling her plate. She took a deep breath and said boldly, "Mother, I have to demand you tell me what is happening with Edmund. Why is his father here? Is he ill? I have to know and if you do not tell me I shall recklessly go to his chambers, alone, to see what is the matter."

Georgina knew that the idea of her arriving at Edmund's chambers without a chaperone would shock her mother. She felt the only way she would get her mother to reveal what was happening was to deliver an ultimatum.

Her mother, always composed, set her cup of tea on the table. "You will do no such thing, miss," she said quietly. "If you even attempt it, you will be met by your uncle, who will be extremely cross. Upon your return here, you would find your bags packed and you would be on your way back to Marksley Manor that very day."

Chapter Seven

Georgina gasped. She had not thought her mother would think to send her home. She should have known she was no match for Lady Marksley.

"What I will tell you, Georgina, so that your mind may be at rest, is that your cousin is in no way indisposed."

"But then why has he not been anywhere? He has not even been here! What can it possibly mean--"

Her mother cut her off. "Enough," her mother said firmly. "And you are not to speak of any of this to Ann. I will not have you worry her. You will see your cousin soon enough and realize that all this worry over him is quite unearned."

Georgina saw that her mother was resolute. At least she had discovered that Edmund was not ill. Though she was instructed not to tell Ann, she reasoned with herself that if her mother knew she had already told Ann that her father was in town and that they had speculated that Edmund might suffer from an illness, then surely her mother would want Ann to know that was not the case.

Dear Ann. Of course she would think her brother must be ill. The only other possibility was that he was in some sort of trouble. What had he done? Was it serious, or was it just some silly hi-jinx?

Georgina once again considered Edmund's temperament. She thought of how Ann had compared him to Lord Greystone. It was true, Edmund was a bit boyish. He was all high spirits and jokes. While Greystone, well, he was all seriousness and condescension. She had never met anyone who made her feel so badly about herself.

Georgina smiled. She really better stop thinking about whether or not she wanted to marry Edmund. He had not shown the slightest hint that he would ask her. The entire idea had sprung forth in her own mind because they got on so well together and it seemed so pleasant to stay the mistress of Marksley Manor after Edmund inherited. As for Greystone, he had his fun with her and that was over. She doubted he would ever approach her for any reason again.

Ann had entered the dining room and Georgina had given her a sign while her mother had not been looking. She would meet Ann in the library as soon as they could get away.

Just as Georgina was hoping she might excuse herself without arousing suspicion, Kingston came in with a note on a silver tray. Lady Marksley picked it up. "It's from Lady Castlereagh, addressed to you, Georgina."

Georgina opened the note with some trepidation. Though she felt more at ease with Lady Castlereagh since the forming of the fever committee, the lady still had the power to fray her nerves.

She read the note out-loud. 'Miss Marksley – we are holding an emergency meeting at Almack's in one hour. Fever has broken out in Whitechapel. Bring Miss Carrington with you.'

Georgina dropped the note. "I was wrong," she said. "My plan has failed."

"Do not jump to conclusions, my dear," her mother said. "It seems to me that if there were not something to be done about it, then there would be no need for a meeting."

"One hour!" Ann cried.

Georgina and Ann had raced to dress themselves. Jemma was cross about it and muttered that Georgina should not tell anyone that Jemma had been responsible for her hair, as she could not be expected to do a creditable job in so short a time.

Georgina had giggled at the idea of arriving at Almack's and discussing who had arranged her hair.

As the carriage raced toward King Street, Ann said, "Your mother was right, you must not assume your plan has failed. Let us see what is said."

It was fine for Ann not to be worried, but her failure would be so public! Everyone knew Georgina was deeply involved in the scheme, even if they did not know exactly what the scheme was. She had been so certain it would work. Where had she gone wrong in her thinking?

They entered the supper room and Georgina quietly slipped into her seat. Sir Halford was in conversation with Lady Castlereagh. Georgina looked around the room and noticed Miss Stanhope glaring at her. What a ridiculous little miss! How did she have the nerve to blame Georgina for the failure when the only idea she'd had was to bring in wind to blow away the noxious fumes?

"We shall begin," Lady Castlereagh said. "Sir Halford will provide us the details of the situation."

"Thank you Lady Castlereagh," he said. He looked sternly around the room. "As usual, no swooning or fan-waving. Now, it appears we have fever broken out on one street in Whitechapel. Somehow, our soldiers missed it."

Missed it? Did that mean her plan *had* worked?

"We believe the improved drainage on the other streets has held back the fever. The question now is; how do we prevent the spread? It's one thing to stop a fever erupting and another to halt one that already exists."

That was true, Georgina thought. Back at the manor, once an illness had appeared it spread quickly and no one, not even the physician, knew how to stop it.

"Whatever we try, we must try quickly," Sir Halford said.

Just then, Lord Greystone swept into the room. "So," he said, unceremoniously, "have we anything yet?"

"Sir Halford has just explained to us," Lady Castlereagh said, "that we have fever on a street the soldiers missed. We understand that Miss Marksley's scheme has been a success, but now we are faced with how to control the spread of the outbreak."

"Yes, yes, of course," Lord Greystone said distractedly.

Georgina could see that Greystone was clearly tired, as if he had been working straight through the days. Despite his unpleasant temperament, he really did have concern for the poor souls who had not escaped the fever. She grudgingly gave him that point.

How could they help? What did they know? Georgina knew that her father always separated a sick cow from the healthy, her father called it a quarantine, and she remembered what Ann had said about how the strong to begin always fared better through an illness. She thought she might have an idea.

"Well?" Lord Greystone said again.

"I might have something," Georgina said quietly. "I really am not sure of it, but it might be something to try."

Lord Greystone stared at her with a penetrating gaze. She really wished he would stop staring. And Miss Stanhope would stop glaring.

"Out with it," Sir Halford cried.

"Yes, of course. Well, perhaps we might try a quarantine on that particular street. I realize it would not be as easy to do with people as it is with cows, but that may also present an opportunity. If we allow no one to enter or leave, then the soldiers will have to supply those people with all their daily wants. We could ensure that they had ample food, because as my cousin has mentioned, the well-fed tend to do better through an illness. In that way, perhaps we could stop the spread, and assist the souls who have already been stricken."

She could see that Lord Greystone approved of her plan. He looked at her admiringly. No doubt it had been on his mind how to help those who had already been stricken.

"Yes," Sir Halford said, "with a few adjustments it might be made to work. We will need soldiers permanently based so that no one leaves. We will need a physician, Doctor Henry would no doubt do it, he's fearless in the face of fever. And there's a pub on the street, we could use that as a sort of headquarters. The one problem I see is wages. These people need to work or they will starve. Even if we could provide compensation for the duration, what after? Many will have lost their positions."

"I'll talk to Prinny about that," Lord Greystone said. "He can order their employers not to dismiss them. I will cover the cost of the wages. And, to ensure that no one attempts to leave, I will give them half wages to begin, and half when the fever is dissipated, plus an extra guinea a man."

Georgina was startled that Lord Greystone had just referred to the Prince of Wales as Prinny. Only his close circle of friends would presume to do so. She could not imagine the serious Greystone and the bon vivant Prince of Wales having anything in common at all. She also thought Greystone must be quite rich – wages and a guinea to what would probably be at least a hundred families was a sizable sum.

Lord Greystone and Sir Halford looked at each other. "We have a lot to do," Sir Halford said.

Greystone nodded.

As they prepared to leave, Lady Castlereagh directed them to send the Almack's committee regular updates. Sir Halford bowed to her. Lord Greystone bowed to Georgina. She felt herself color.

Miss Stanhope, as she seemed to be always doing recently, gave Georgina an icy stare.

"Well done, Georgi," her mother said. It was the following afternoon and they were in the sitting room in Berkeley Square having tea.

"She really is so very clever," Ann said.

"Now, Ann," Georgina said, "half the idea was yours, remember? I just borrowed it."

"Congratulations to both of you, then," Lady Marksley said. "You have represented the family well." Lady Marksley paused. Then she said, "You know we are to dine in this evening. Edmund and Sir Carrington will join us. I bring this up now because they will have an announcement of sorts. I would ask both of you to quietly listen. Do not question, just accept what you have heard with grace and continue on with polite table conversation. Now, I will retire to my room and rest."

Lady Marksley swept from the room.

"An announcement of sorts?" Georgina asked Ann. "Certainly Edmund would not come to announce he is ill, so I fear he must be in some sort of trouble."

"I am afraid you are right," Ann said. "Oh, Edmund! What have you done?"

"Perhaps it is not so terribly bad," Georgina said, hopefully. "He may have just gotten into some silly scrape." Though she said it, Georgina was not sure she believed it. Her mother and her uncle had been a bit too mysterious thus far to account for a minor infraction.

"Whatever it is we are to hear," Ann said, "we must do exactly as your mother has directed us to do. No matter how shocking, we will not show our feelings on what is said. We will let it pass by quickly, and then carry on with our dinner."

Georgina knew it would take every ounce of self-control to avoid asking a hundred questions. She had not even heard anything yet and she was full of them. Where had Edmund been? Why had he not called on them in so long?

Georgina had a sudden idea that had not occurred to her before now. One that might settle her feelings for Edmund once and for all. She could not decide if she would be happy or sad about that. "Ann," she said, "perhaps it is not what we think. Perhaps Edmund will announce an engagement."

Ann was pensive. Then she said, "But why the secrecy? And why should we not comment on it when it is announced? Unless…the girl is unsuitable in some way?"

"Or perhaps the marriage has already taken place?" Georgina said.

"Gretna Green!" Ann exclaimed. "Oh no, he would not. Not even Edmund would be so foolish."

"Perhaps it was…necessary?"

Ann held her hands over her ears. "Do not, Georgina, do not even think it!"

Georgina did not want to think it, but she could not help it. What else but a marriage would warrant an announcement? One did not announce they were ill, or announce they had accrued a large gambling debt, or announce they had been running with a wild crowd. All the things Georgina had speculated Edmund had done did not require announcements. Only a marriage merited an announcement.

There was every possibility that Edmund had put some tradesman's daughter in a family way and then gone and married her.

Edmund could be rash beyond words, but she had seen him act kindly. Georgina did not think he would leave such a girl in the lurch. But oh! The shame that would come down upon them all when it was known!

Georgina could just imagine the look on Lord Greystone's face when he heard of it. The man already did not like her cousin, he would revel in his fall.

And Lady Castlereagh! Georgina feared that would be the end of her association with Almack's.

Another, graver, concern flashed across Georgina's mind. Marriage. For all the balls and parties and committee work, the real reason she was in London was to find a suitable husband. Depending on how far Edmund's fall from grace actually was, she might find herself standing at the edge of the ballroom in want of a partner as all the young men began to look elsewhere. Or worse, she would not even be invited to the balls at all. What shame it would be to sit here day after day, as the post brought no invitations.

But perhaps she was being too melodramatic. After all, Edmund may have just been reckless. He may have run off with some respectable girl. It was true that eloping would cause a scandal, but not an un-survivable one if the two families could be brought together to patch the whole thing up. The couple would be thought quite romantic. Georgina would certainly lose her voucher to Almack's, but there were plenty of marriageable girls who had never had a voucher to begin. Almack's was not the only venue for seeking a husband.

She must just hope that the situation that Edmund had placed them in was not too dire. Georgina blushed as she thought of all those times she had considered marrying Edmund. While she was daydreaming, he was off pursuing someone else.

Georgina turned to her cousin. Poor Ann! She would take the brunt of the scandal, whatever it was. As much as she had been against Ann marrying Sir Langston, now she was all for it. Sir Langston would likely not blink at the thing, whatever it was. He was a stalwart, sensible man and it was clear he was smitten with Ann.

Ann, for her part, sat staring morosely into the fire. Georgina rose from her chair and knelt by her side. She took her hand and said, "Dear Ann, whatever it is, we shall face it together. You have been my steady anchor all these many years and now I will be yours."

The afternoon loomed long and tense as Georgina waited for the time to arrive when they would hear all. She was a bundle of unspent energy. Ann had composed herself and sat reading quietly, though Georgina had her doubts that much was read, as Ann had not turned a page in the past half hour.

Georgina finally decided she would go for a ride. If she did not, she might well explode.

Georgina trotted her horse down the lady's mile, with her groom following behind. She passed many acquaintance, who tipped their hats and called good day. For now, whatever Edmund had done was unknown. Georgina felt a pang of something lost as she realized that very soon, many of those faces might be turned away from her. Why must a girl be so affected by her relations? It hardly seemed fair. Of course, she knew why. No man wanted to be tied to a scandalous family forevermore.

"Miss Marksley," she heard from behind her. She recognized the voice instantly and had a great urge to send Juno into a gallop.

"Miss Marksley," Lord Greystone said, trotting alongside her.

"Oh," she said. "It's you, Lord Greystone." Georgina thought that might be one of the stupidest things she had ever said. Who else would it be? Greystone had not seemed to notice.

"Sir Halford and I have accomplished much since yesterday. The perimeter of the fever-stricken area has been secured and its residents are under the care of a physician. I suspect you will have saved many lives."

Lord Greystone had that same look on his face that Georgina had noticed the day before. It was some sort of mix of friendly, approving admiration. Oh, why did he have to approve of her now? It would make whatever fall from grace that loomed ahead that much more awful.

She should not care about his opinion at all. Why did she, then? Certainly, Georgina had to admit, she did care.

"I'm very pleased to hear it," she said softly.

"Will you attend the Fairfield's rout this evening?" he asked.

"Oh," she stammered, "no. I have a…family engagement. My cousin and my uncle are coming to dine."

Lord Greystone's face settled into hard lines.

What was the meaning of it? He could not know anything of Edmund's disgrace yet.

He tipped his hat and said, "Good day, Miss Marksley."

Georgina watched him canter away. She could not make any sense out of that man. She sighed to herself. There was no point trying to unravel her feelings about Lord Greystone. Whatever regard he held her in for her work on the committee would be dashed to pieces soon enough. Then, she suspected, he would pretend they had never met.

Chapter Eight

The hour had finally come. Edmund and Georgina's uncle had arrived at the house and the conversation in the drawing room had been stilted and awkward. It was all so strange. Usually Edmund would be the life of the room, joking and laughing. Now though, he avoided meeting her eye. Whatever he had done, he was embarrassed for her to know it.

They finally went in to dine.

The dining room had been set up. When it was only Lady Marksley, Ann and Georgina, they ate in the breakfast room at a more intimate table, as Lord Marksley invariably ate at his club. Their meals were simple with just one soup and two meats. However,

Georgina knew her uncle loved a good table and Lady Marksley had certainly made an effort to please him.

The room was well-lit with candles; the table could easily afford thirty guests. The footmen had set the table at one end, though they had laid the cloth across the whole. They would have a full four meats and Georgina knew that her mother had even had venison brought in from the estate.

The time the servants took to serve the soup seemed interminable. Georgina knew that whatever would be said, Kingston would hear it. He would stand by in case anyone should need more wine or assistance of some sort. He could be trusted with any family secret, but nothing would be said until the footmen were sent away.

The last of the footmen left, closing the door behind him. Kingston stood in the corner of the room, ramrod straight and staring off into space as if he had no ability to hear what was said.

Finally, her uncle said to Ann and Georgina, "You may well wonder why I did not announce my arrival back in town."

There was silence at the table. Of course they had wondered, though there did not seem to be anything to say about it.

"As it happens," her uncle continued, "Edmund and I had some business to discuss. He will return to the country with me. He will not be in town again this year."

"He is not married?" Georgina cried.

"Married?" Edmund said. He looked at her as if she had gone mad.

Her father gave her a sharp look.

"Georgina!" her mother said. "Enough."

The rest of the dinner passed by in a blur. Georgina was sure she had answered questions from her uncle about where she had been and who she had met over the past month, but she remembered none of it. Edmund was not married. Whatever trouble he was in, he had not run off to Gretna Green. He stole glances at her from time to time, clearly shocked that she had thought it.

This new Edmund, more serious than she had ever seen him, made her like him more than ever. Whatever he had done, it clearly was not the ruin of them all and perhaps it had been just the scare Edmund had needed to thrust him out of boyhood and into manhood. Georgina thought he had probably lost too large a sum gambling and had to call upon his father to settle the debt. She could easily imagine her uncle insisting he come home for the duration of the season as a punishment. Why hadn't that occurred to her in the first place? All those silly imaginings of race to Gretna Green and an unsuitable marriage!

Whatever had happened, it appeared to Georgina that she was safe from ruin. Her heart lightened and threw off all its heavy worries. She would not have to dread encountering Lord Greystone.

Georgina paused. Again, when she thought of other's opinions, she had thought of his first. He was not casual and carefree, like so many of the other gentleman were. Somehow, because his good opinion was harder to get, it meant more.

Careful Georgina, she said to herself. You are in danger of beginning to like the man.

Usually, a family dinner would stretch long into the night. They would repair to the drawing room and Georgina and Ann would take turns at the piano, or perhaps she and Edmund would battle on the chess board. This evening, her uncle hustled Edmund out the door directly after dinner. There was barely time to say goodbye.

Georgina had sidled over to her mother after they had gone, hoping Lady Marksley would finally explain the mystery of what Edmund had done, but her mother had said, "Nothing further, Georgina," and retired to her room.

Georgina and Ann stayed in the drawing room and talked long into the night about Edmund's appearance, and his manner at dinner and speculated on whatever could have happened.

As the candles burned low, Ann said, "I must say I agree with you, Georgina. I have never seen my brother so subdued."

"But at least there was no unsuitable marriage announced," Georgina said. "We shall not end up the talk of London."

Ann shivered. "Thank heavens for that."

"Ann," Georgina said. "You must write your brother and find out what has happened. I know you are very strict about following your parent's wishes, but no one has said you cannot write. He's your brother, after all. It would be the most natural thing to write him. And you need not ask him about it directly. You may just leave enough room in your questions for him to tell you."

"I believe I will do that," Ann said. "You are right, no one has told me not to. As you say, I will not ask him directly, but if he wishes he may tell me."

The following week, Georgina received a note from Lady Castlereagh that an Almack's meeting was called. She did not know whether to look forward to it or dread it. It must be known by now how the quarantine fared. She had not heard of the fever spreading, so she had every hope that it had been a success.

In the Almack's supper room, Georgina sat nervously, waiting for Lady Castlereagh to begin. Lady Castlereagh was composed and silent at the head of the table. Georgina began to get the feeling she was waiting for someone, and as she glanced around the room and saw all the girls accounted for, she thought she could probably guess who.

The thought of seeing Lord Greystone again gave her a slightly giddy feeling. At their last meeting, she had been sure she would be disgraced the following day. That hadn't happened, and she could hold her head high in any company, including his.

Georgina paused. In the terror of wondering what Edmund had done, Georgina had quite forgotten Greystone's odd reaction when she had said she would stay home for a family dinner. What had he meant by it? He could not possibly despise Edmund so much that he was irritated that Edmund's own family chose to dine with him.

Lord Greystone and Sir Halford strode into the room.

Georgina felt herself blush and scolded herself for being such a ninny.

"Ladies," Sir Halford began, "our quarantine has been a success. There has been no new fever reported in the city for over a week. The people who were struck with it on the affected block have been under the care of a physician and are doing remarkably well. He has advised dosing them with hearty bone broths to good effect." Sir Halford bowed in Georgina's direction and said, "Bravo, Miss Marksley."

Lord Greystone was practically beaming. He turned to Georgina and said, "In honor of the accomplishments of the Almack's committee, Prinny, I mean the Prince of Wales, will throw a ball one week from today at Carlton House. The committee will serve as the guests of honor. You will receive formal invitations from the Prince."

The girls around the table gasped. Georgina gasped with them. They were to be honored at a ball? By the Prince of Wales himself?

She could only imagine what her mother would say. Lady Marksley would be half-thrilled that her daughter received such an honor, and half-terrified to let her daughter anywhere near the Prince.

Lady Castlereagh stood and said to Lord Greystone, "Tell the prince that the Almack's committee is honored by his notice." She turned to the girls and said, "And I second Sir Halford. Bravo Miss Marksley."

Georgina felt the flush across her cheeks. If this were to go on much longer, she would turn positively purple. She noticed Lord Greystone was flushed too. Good Lord, why were they both blushing? She wanted to stamp her foot and make it stop.

Finally, Sir Halford and Lord Greystone made their departure. Tea was sent for and Georgina was glad to escape as the center of attention. She sat with Ann as Miss Stanhope approached them. Miss Stanhope glanced over her shoulder to Lady Castlereagh, who was deep in conversation with Lady Worthington. She bent forward and whispered in Georgina's ear.

"Aren't you the clever one," she hissed.

Georgina pulled back, startled. Miss Stanhope had stalked off.

"What in the world?" Georgina said. Of course, she was fairly certain what in the world had gotten into Miss Stanhope. She did not like Lord Greystone's attention away from her one bit.

Georgina leaned toward Ann and said softly, "I really should tell her that there is not, and will never be, anything between myself and Lord Greystone."

"Would that be quite right, Georgina?" Ann said, with a mischievous smile. "It is not nice to tell fibs."

"What?" Georgina said.

"You know perfectly well, what. There's something there. I do not know what, exactly, but he is not indifferent to you." Ann paused and said, "And I think you are not indifferent to him."

"Ann!" Georgina said, a bit louder than she meant to. She lowered her voice. "There is nothing, absolutely nothing, between us.

There is less than nothing! We barely tolerate each other, and only for the good of the committee."

"Come now," Ann said. "I think your view of him has changed as you become more acquainted. It seems you have quite given up calling him names."

Georgina paused. That was true, she had stopped calling him Lord Gloom. Was there something there? Even if she were prevailed upon to like him, she was quite sure it would not be returned. They were too dissimilar, and Greystone despised her cousin Edmund, and his family surely expected him to bring home a bride who was the daughter of a Duke or an Earl, not a lowly Viscount. There was simply everything against it.

And yet, he did have those stormy grey eyes that were hard to ignore.

No, she would dismiss the idea from her mind immediately. What she should be considering is who among her acquaintance might be a real suitor. And Edmund. Was there anything with

Edmund? She did not know, but she was eager to see if his new-found maturity would stick. If it did, he might well think of taking a wife. He might well think of asking Georgina.

Poor Edmund – he would miss the ball at Carlton House. At the thought of being a guest of honor of the Prince of Wales, Georgina felt a little faint. She had grown comfortable running with her own crowd, but this would be different. What would she wear? How would she be judged? She knew the Prince's set was ruthless and could cut a person down to size.

Georgina fanned herself at the thought of being scrutinized by Mr. Beau Brummel. Would she pass his merciless gaze, or become the subject of some joke from the witty man? Would he find her acceptable or dismiss her as another country bumpkin lately to town?

There was so much to think about that Georgina felt she would be better off not thinking about anything at all.

The sitting room in Berkeley Square was cozy and bright against the fog at the windows. The weather had been warm and fine until that afternoon. A spring storm had thundered over London, bringing in cooler air.

"Carlton House?" Lady Marksley said, sounding alarmed.

"Yes, mother," Georgina answered. "But I'm quite sure you will be invited as well - Lady Castlereagh will arrange that. And we shall be quite safe under the gaze of the Patronesses."

"I suppose so," her mother said. "It certainly is an honor for your committee. I'm sure Lady Castlereagh was pleased."

"Although the honor is ostensibly for the committee," Ann said, "the real honor is Georgina's."

"Oh please, Ann," Georgina cried. "I cannot bear to blush one more time today."

"What in heaven's name have you been blushing about, Georgi?" her mother asked.

"Well," Georgina stammered. "Everything. Being stared at by…everybody. Lady Castlereagh, and the other girls…"

"And Sir Halford and Lord Greystone," Ann added helpfully.

"Ah," her mother said, seeming pleased. "Lord Greystone."

Georgina would have liked to disappear into her chair. She would scold Ann severely for teasing her so.

Her mother saw her discomfort and said, "There, there, girl. Never mind. We have more important tasks at hand. We shall go directly to the dressmaker tomorrow morning. Both of you shall have new gowns."

The next week was a whirlwind of preparation. Invitations from the Prince of Wales arrived for Georgina, Ann and Lady Marksley. Material was selected for the gowns. Georgina had her heart set on a dark green silk she had seen in the dressmaker's shop, but her mother had refused. Lady Marksley insisted on a delicate rose and said it would be more befitting a young girl in her first season about to attend a ball thrown by the Prince of Wales. Ann chose a pale yellow silk for herself. Gloves and ribbons and every kind of frippery were purchased. Fittings were had, and Georgina was glad her mother had prevailed, the color of the gown cast her skin in a rosy glow.

The day of the ball arrived. Lady Marksley had instructed Georgina and Ann to lay abed as long as possible and breakfast in their rooms so that they might be well-rested for the evening's gaiety. Georgina was fidgety and could not stay in bed, so she took a cup of tea and slice of buttered toast and tiptoed down the hall to Ann's room.

She tapped lightly on the door.

"Good morning, Georgina," Ann called. "Do come in."

Georgina slipped through the door. "How did you ever know it was me?" she asked.

Ann laughed. "When Lady Marksley told us to stay abed, I wondered how you would manage it. Then I decided you would probably not manage it."

Georgina set her tea and slice of toast on a side table and threw herself in an overstuffed chair by the window. She hugged her knees and breathed in the fine air of the morning breeze coming through the open window. "You know me too well, Ann. Now, how should we pass this interminable day until we leave for Carlton House?"

Ann sipped her tea, then said, "Truly, I do not know. I am usually not nervous about attending a ball, it generally feels to me like one more chore to be got through, but on this occasion I feel quite high-strung."

"Do you really dislike balls so much? That they feel like a chore?" Georgina asked.

"It's not that I dislike them exactly, it's just that this whole London season seems so…"

"So not where Sir Langston happens to be?"

"Georgina!" Ann cried.

"Take no offense, my dear," Georgina said. "I've quite resigned myself to the match. Though you could have Lord Tansby in a moment if you liked. I believe he is quite taken with you."

"Georgina! Stop this instant," Ann said.

"But Ann, how lucky you are," Georgina said. "To truly like someone! I do not know if I will ever…" Georgina trailed off. It was true that of late, she had begun to think of Ann as lucky. She hadn't thought it when they had arrived in London. She had rather more pitied her cousin than not. Ann of the pin-straight hair and the landed gentry suitor. Then, Georgina had thought she was the luckiest girl in the world, not Ann. But now she saw that, however much Ann refused to talk about it, her feelings were steady for Sir Langston. Georgina's feelings were anything but steady. Did she want to marry Edmund or not? Had Edmund thought of marrying her or not? Was he really changed into a man from whatever scrape he had gotten himself into? Was there anything in Ann's speculation about herself and Lord Greystone? Greystone would be at the ball, perhaps Georgina could put her mind to rest on that point at least. That was assuming he asked her to dance.

"Why are you blushing, Georgina? You are as red as St. Nick."

"Am I?" she said. She turned her face to the window. "It must be the morning breeze."

Carlton House was magnificent. The Prince had recently remodeled it and it was an homage to all things French and exotic. The ball itself would be held in the crimson drawing room. The chairs had been removed and Georgina tried not to gawk at the ornate vaulted ceiling in silver and gold and the floor to ceiling red draperies. It was small by ballroom standards and Georgina instantly realized that this ball would not be the usual crush of people. It appeared to her as though it was comprised solely of the ladies and gentleman who had worked on the fever committees and the Prince of Wales' close acquaintance.

This idea sent a shiver through Georgina. As much as she wanted to meet the Prince of Wales, she was terrified too. But the Prince was nothing compared to Mr. Brummel. That man could make a girl the laughingstock of London by issuing one clever bon mot that would be repeated endlessly in every drawing room in town. The year before, as Georgina sat in the country reading a letter from her friend Clara Cambridge, she had laughed at the plight of a certain Miss Jennings. It appeared that Miss Jennings had been overly enthusiastic in her use of ribbons and Mr. Brummel was heard to say, "She would be able to tie up Napoleon's army with those yards." Miss Jennings promptly relocated back to the country rather than be a source of constant amusement. Now, Georgina deeply regretted her laughter over Miss Jennings. She could only pray that Mr. Brummel would either not see her at all, or think her too unremarkable to talk about.

"Miss Marksley."

Georgina came back from her musings to find Lord Wainsworth standing in front of her. She curtsied.

"May I have the first set?" he asked.

"Yes, of course," Georgina said. That was one bright spot, she thought. She had danced with Lord Wainsworth many times before. He was a skilled and graceful dancer and she knew she would look well as his partner.

Lord Wainsworth bowed and retreated, no doubt to line up a partner for his second set. Georgina smiled. It was well noted around town that Lord Wainsworth never missed a ball and never sat out a set. No one would find him standing idly by or sitting at a card table.

Ann whispered behind her fan. "Lord Greystone, striding in your direction and looking as determined as ever."

Georgina colored, then scolded herself for doing it. Why did the man make her so nervous? He was of no higher rank than Lord Wainsworth and Georgina did not have the slightest bit of nerves near him.

Lord Greystone bowed. "Miss Marksley."

Georgina curtsied. "Lord Greystone."

Lord Greystone acknowledged Ann, then he said to Georgina, "May I have the first set?"

"Oh," Georgina said, feeling a bit pleased to be already engaged, "I am sorry, I am already engaged by Lord Wainsworth."

"I see," he said, a cloud passing over his features. "The second, then?"

"Yes," Georgina said quietly.

Lord Greystone hurried away, looking a bit put out. Georgina was beginning to believe Ann's opinion of Greystone's interest in her. Ann was right, he did appear determined. Could it be that he regretted his rude behavior when they first met? But then, why had he not apologized for it? Perhaps she had not given him the chance? And even so, even if Ann was right, what did she think about it? He was handsome, there was no denying that. He had the finest pair of eyes of any gentleman in town. But his temperament. Was he not too serious for her? Part of her said that it was so, and yet another part of her felt not quite as indisposed to seriousness as she had been when she first arrived in town.

Miss Stanhope swept into the room, a vision of blond curls and pale blue silk. Georgina had to admit, somewhat ruefully, that she was particularly pretty. Georgina watched Greystone approach her. Clearly he had asked for the first set and she had accepted. After he departed, Miss Stanhope caught Georgina's eye and smiled triumphantly. Georgina giggled at the thought of how angry Miss Stanhope would be to find she had come in second place.

Georgina froze. Mr. Brummel had entered the ballroom. He was tall and elegant and wore a snowy white cravat tied in a style Georgina had never seen before. He strolled to Miss Stanhope, bowed and said "Charmed." He walked by Miss Cavendish and Miss Templeton without acknowledging them. He glanced over Ann's head as if she did not exist. He stopped in front of Georgina.

She held her breath and looked down. She could not meet his eye; she could only pray he was not about to send her the way of Miss Jennings.

Chapter Nine

Mr. Brummel lifted Georgina's chin with the tip of his quizzing glass. He said, "A rose-colored dress for an English rose. Charming." He walked off and Georgina felt flooded with relief. Mr. Brummel would not destroy her every chance for happiness.

Lady Marksley held her fan up and said to Georgina, "I told you the rose silk was the right choice."

"So you did, mother," Georgina said with real gratefulness in her voice. "You did."

The musicians struck up. Ann was led away by Lord Bedford and Georgina was led to the dance floor by Lord Wainsworth. The Prince of Wales would open the dance with Lady Castlereagh.

Georgina supposed that the Prince gave Lady Castlereagh all the credit for staving off the fever. She thought that was quite all right. She would probably faint if she were put on the spot in front of the Prince and, after all, it was Lady Castlereagh that had formed the committee.

Georgina was relieved to find she was not dancing the cotillion with the Prince's couples, but vexed that Lord Greystone and Miss Stanhope were part of her own couples. She had hoped to be at her ease while she danced with Lord Wainsworth, but now she would be faced with the staring Greystone and glaring Miss Stanhope.

Lord Wainsworth was full of amusing anecdotes, including one told in three parts about his steward and a wayward horse. As she went through the changes, Georgina could not help but notice Greystone staring at her. She willed him to stop it, as Miss Stanhope had clearly noticed. She did not particularly like Miss Stanhope, but Georgina would not like to find herself in the same position.

The set ended and Lord Wainsworth escorted her to the punch bowl. As she sipped the Negus, she was startled to hear Lord Wainsworth say, "Miss Marksley, may I present the Prince of Wales."

Georgina deeply curtsied. The Prince raised her up. "I understand from Lady Castlereagh that you were the clever girl that stopped the fever."

Georgina felt that her face must now match the color of her dress. "Please, your royal highness, it was Lady Castlereagh who formed the committee. She must be given the credit."

"Ah," the Prince said, "and modest too. Very charming girl."

The prince moved on to greet other guests. Georgina felt as light as a soap bubble. She had survived it all. Mr. Brummel's scrutiny and an introduction to the Prince of Wales and she had not embarrassed herself.

Lord Wainsworth leaned over and said, "Prinny is nothing but gracious. As you see, he does not care a whit about that business with your cousin."

Georgina froze. "What business," she said quietly.

Lord Wainsworth colored from his cravat to his forehead. "Pardon me," he stammered.

"Lord Wainsworth," Georgina said firmly. "We have danced dozens of times; we know each other too well to be coy. Please tell me what you refer to."

Lord Wainsworth paused, seeming to consider whether he ought to say more. Finally, he said, "Just the thing about the card game. Greystone caught him and Brook's threw him out. I had assumed as his cousin you knew."

"Caught him doing what?" Georgina said. Though she had asked the question, she already knew the answer. There was only one thing a gentleman could be 'caught' doing at a card game. Cheating. And he was thrown out of his club! No wonder Edmund's father had come to take him home. A gentleman cheating at cards was socially through.

Georgina paused. None of this could be right. Whatever foolishness Edmund ever got up to, he would never cheat at cards. She knew he would not. He was a gentleman through and through.

Then Georgina remembered the cold greeting between Edmund and Greystone in the park. She suddenly understood it all. Greystone had set her cousin up. Edmund was falsely accused and Greystone was believed. She had known all along that there was something vindictive in Greystone's nature. Whatever bad blood was between them, Greystone had decided to end it by ruining her cousin's reputation.

Georgina felt the sting of tears in her eyes. Edmund could never come back to town. A gentleman without a club was like a gentleman without clothes. How far had the story spread? Georgina had not noticed any slacking off of invitations to herself and Ann, so most likely it was contained amongst the members of Brook's. How long it would be so, she could not guess.

Her mother! Lady Marksley must have known all. But if so, how could she believe it? Why hadn't Edmund's father taken up the fight for him instead of hurrying him back to the country? Why hadn't Edmund, himself, challenged Greystone to a duel? Why would they just allow the man to win? It was all so unfair!

Well, Georgina thought, if the story was spread about, she would defend her cousin and denounce Lord Greystone at every opportunity. If no one would fight for Edmund, she would.

"Miss Marksley."

Lord Greystone stood before her with his hand out. She had completely forgotten he had engaged her for the second set. She could not do it. She just could not.

Georgina ran from the ballroom, looking for some quiet corner to hide until she could gather her thoughts. She had stood up Lord Greystone and made an indecorous exit, but she did not care. Let them all talk.

She found herself in the conservatory. It was empty, though lit with a hundred wax candles. It was a long stretch of hall with a black and white tiled floor and gold columns lining its sides. In other circumstances, Georgina would probably have thought it quite stunning. On this night, she was just glad it was empty.

Georgina paced the length of it, anger growing within her at every step. Why did she have to be female? If she were a man, she would challenge Greystone to a duel and promptly shoot his head off.

"Miss Marksley," Lord Greystone said. He stood at the entrance to the conservatory, appearing out of breath. "What is the matter? Are you ill?"

"Why have you followed me?" she cried. "Why?"

Lord Greystone approached her. "You ran away and I thought, well I was concerned…"

"You were concerned?" Georgina said, white hot anger coursing through her. "You have falsely accused my cousin and he is ruined and now you are concerned? Well, hear this Lord Greystone, you are a sanctimonious prig with a vindictive streak. If you imagine, for one moment, that I would dance with the man who has so wronged my cousin, then you are also very stupid."

"Your cousin? You were never to know. No one was to know-_"

"I am sure I was not meant to know of your misdeeds, but as it happens, I do know. I'm glad I know. My first instincts about you were correct. Further, when this story gets about, I will denounce you all over town. It is about time the ton had a look at the real you."

"I see," Lord Greystone said in a cold and reserved tone. "Good evening, Miss Marksley."

Lord Greystone turned on his heel and strode from the room.

Georgina burst into tears.

The next weeks were tedious and painful. Georgina went through the motions, attending balls and routs and dinner parties, but she enjoyed none of it. Each time she entered a drawing room, she braced herself for icy stares. She knew it would happen sooner or later. Edmund's supposed disgrace would make the rounds and it would be the beginning of the end. She would attend whatever invitations she had already received and nobody would say a word about it. But none new would arrive. She would leave cards, and no one would ever be at home. She and her family would be slowly shut out until there was nowhere to go and no one to call on. What could she do about it? To defend Edmund now would just hasten the story on its rounds. To wait until it was well known would just result in not having the opportunity to defend him, as she would not be invited anywhere. Georgina felt the injustice of it tearing her apart.

Ann had been deeply shocked when she had heard the accusation of cheating and, like Georgina, could not believe it of Edmund. She was less sure of why Lord Greystone would fabricate such a tale. Georgina was of the firm opinion that Edmund and Lord Greystone had some sort of quarrel and Lord Greystone's vindictive nature had authored the rest. Ann said she had not witnessed any signs of vindictiveness, or any other unsavory trait from Lord Greystone and thought perhaps there had been some unfortunate misunderstanding. They spent hours together talking of what might be done about it. All they could manage to conclude was that if they had the opportunity to defend Edmund, they would do so heartily.

Georgina sat listlessly in the sitting room while Ann read her post and her mother worked on an embroidery piece.

Her mother laid her embroidery down. "I almost feel I should call for the physician, Georgi. You look so tired these days. Not at all like your usual self."

"I'm fine, mother," Georgina said. "I think it is just that the season is more grueling than I had imagined."

Out of the corner of her eye, Georgina noticed Ann's hands were shaking as she perused a letter. She laid it on her lap and stared at Georgina.

Edmund! It must be a letter from Edmund. He had finally answered Ann's letter of so many weeks ago.

"I think I shall take a turn in the library, mother. A walk is all I need."

"Very well," Lady Marksley said.

"I shall go with you, Georgina," Ann said. "There's a book in there I've been meaning to read."

They repaired to the library and sat in their special corner.

"It is from Edmund, is it not?" Georgina asked.

"It is," Ann answered. "Though I hardly know what to make of it and I am not entirely sure I should show you."

"You must show me!" Georgina said. "It is you and I that will pay the price for this entire situation."

"That is true," Ann said. "You have every right to know the circumstances. I only hope you will find some way to forgive my brother."

"Forgive him? For being falsely accused? There is nothing to forgive!"

Ann handed her the letter. "You will think otherwise very shortly."

Georgina unfolded the vellum with shaking hands and read the letter.

My dearest sister Ann,

Forgive me for not responding to your letter for so long. I will admit I have avoided doing so and have left it on my night-table these many weeks. As you know, dear one, I despise anything unpleasant and this will be unpleasant indeed. I only write to you now because I fear that my reason for being in the country may reach your ears somehow. I would not want you to hear the story from anyone but myself.

I will just come out with it. I cheated at a game of cards and was caught. I know you are deeply shocked by reading that line. There can be no real excuse for it, but I will try to excuse myself as best I can. Prior to the card game, I had made some very foolish bets and was deeply in debt. I then discovered that the inheritance that I am to receive when I become Lord Marksley is quite smaller than I had anticipated, as a large piece is to be part of Georgina's dowry. I could get no loan against future income to pay the debts I owed.

Ann, if I could not pay my debts I would have been drummed out of Brook's. I felt much as a cornered rat and desperately searched for a solution. One night, I saw my chance at the card table. I will not go into detail about what I did, it hardly matters. My actions were seen by Lord Greystone.

In that moment, I felt my life to be over. But there was a reprieve. Greystone told me he would not reveal my secret if I agreed never to play cards at Brook's again. I immediately acquiesced and, for a time, I felt I had escaped the hangman's noose.

Oh Ann, if only I had learned my lesson! That incident should have sobered me, but instead, I began to look on it as some sort of joke. My life had continued on, unscathed, and I forgot the initial fear of being caught. That is when I truly became the author of my own destruction. One evening, quite in my cups I'm sorry to say, I revealed what happened to my friend, Gallaway. At least, I had thought he was my friend. The next morning, I found the entire club knew of it and I was on my way out.

If it is any consolation to you at all, I am hopeful that this story will not make the rounds. Greystone had every member of Brook's, even Prinny himself, sign an oath that they would never reveal the circumstances of my departure. I only pray they stand by their word.

As for my future, I hope to win Georgina's hand and hope you will help me. Keeping her dowry as part of the estate will make life much more comfortable and I am sure you will like to see me married and settled. As it is, I have few options. If I come to town for another season it will be noted that I no longer belong to Brook's. I would not like that to reflect badly on you dear Ann, so you must help me with Georgina, you see?

Again, I hope you can forgive your very foolish brother.

Warmest, Edmund.

Georgina dropped the vellum and watched it fall to the floor. Edmund had not been falsely accused. Greystone had even tried to protect him!

The scene in the conservatory rolled through her mind. All the hateful things she had said. And his so very cold departure. He had known the real truth of it and she had not. She remembered he had even said that no one was to know about it. What a stupid girl she was.

All this time, she had been ready to defend Edmund far and wide, when he deserved no such thing. And he would presume to get her hand to hold on to her dowry and nearly blackmail Ann into helping him?

Georgina felt as if she had never known the real Edmund. She had been taken in by all the gaiety and fun and had not seen the callous, immoral man underneath the laughter.

Ann sat quietly, a single tear running down her cheek. "You see why I did not know if I should show you the letter, Georgina. Filled as it is with the scandalous truth, what I find more shocking is his designs on you. It is so…cold and calculating. I had always hoped my brother would grow out of his self-indulgence but, as you can see, it is only his own comfort he cares for."

Georgina patted Ann's hand. "It is not your fault that he is as he is. Never fear, he will never convince me to marry him after all of this. I am quite safe."

"But for him to attempt to drag me into such a scheme! How could he think it of me?"

"As you said yourself, Ann, he only thinks of his own comfort. How you would feel about it probably never occurred to him. Oh," Georgina said, hugging her cousin, "but what a good friend you are. I know I shall always be safe in your hands."

"Georgina," Ann said, "what of Lord Greystone?"

"What of Lord Greystone," Georgina said ruefully. "I have insulted him thoroughly and unjustly and will never have the opportunity to apologize because he has avoided me as if I carried plague ever since the Prince's ball. Have you not noted that we no longer see him anywhere? I am sure that is my doing. Well, your brother may not have learned his lesson, but I have learned mine. I will no longer be so quick to judge people and assume I understand their motives. I have been thoroughly schooled."

"Still, there might come an opportunity to say something. He is bound to turn up somewhere," Ann said. "You could very well find him sitting next to you at a dinner. You do like him, do you not, Georgina?"

Did she? She had been so angry with him, casting him as the blackest villain. Now she saw that was wrong. He had been nothing but honorable. It was not just Edmund she began to see in a new light. Greystone had made the gentleman of the club, even the Prince of Wales, sign an oath not to reveal Edmund's disgrace. Had that been for her benefit? She doubted it had been for Edmund's.

Greystone had taken her thoughts on preventing the fever seriously. It now occurred to her that Edmund had never taken her seriously about anything. He had laughed off ideas she'd had from books she'd read and told her not to worry her pretty head over such deep subjects.

Georgina shivered at the thought of how many hours she had spent considering Edmund as a husband. Had he not been caught cheating at cards, she might very well have married him and discovered later that he had been only interested in her dowry. On top of everything else, Greystone had unwittingly saved her from a life of misery.

"I hardly think it matters whether or not I like Lord Greystone," Georgina said to Ann. "Thanks to my sharp tongue, that ship has quite left the harbor."

"I wish there were more I could do," Ann said. "However, I can at least do what is in my power. I shall answer my brother's letter in no uncertain terms. I will let him know you have read it, and that should end his designs on you."

Chapter Ten

The next week was all dreariness. The rain poured down on London as if the Gods were wringing out the clouds. It was impossible to go out, the streets were flooded and the fog had descended, enveloping Berkeley Square in a damp, grey blanket. Day after day, Georgina sat next to the sitting room fire, pretending to read a book. She occasionally turned a page so that her mother would not grow suspicious.

She did not read one word of it. Rather, she spent her days reliving all that had happened in the last months.

Georgina had arrived in London so confident. She had felt ready to take on the town. Now, she saw herself more clearly. She was just a young country bumpkin, stumbling from one mistake to the next.

Georgina had not understood Edmund's character at all. It made her blush to remember that her mother had seemed clear about Edmund all along. Even before the scandal, Lady Marksley had not approved of him and was against a match. Georgina had felt herself so much smarter than her mother, and now she saw it was not so.

Georgina had not understood Lord Greystone's character either. When she examined the facts, except for him failing to acknowledge her when she nearly bowled him over with her horse, which given the circumstances she knew now was perfectly understandable, what other crime had he committed? While Edmund was racking up debt and cheating at cards, Greystone was trying to save lives from the fever. She had no doubt now that he had worked tirelessly with Sir Halford to enact her schemes.

Georgina felt herself a perfect idiot. She was meant to come to London and find a suitable husband. A handsome Earl of good character had taken an interest in her. In return, she had shouted at him like a fishwife.

Kingston interrupted her thoughts. He held a silver platter with a card out to her mother.

"Someone is calling? In this weather?" Lady Marksley said, picking up the card. "Good gracious. It's Lady Castlereagh."

Lady Castlereagh? Why would Lady Castlereagh venture out in this downpour? Georgina's heart sank. Somehow, Edmund's shame had reached her ears. She could feel in her very bones that Lady Castlereagh had come to ask for the Almack's voucher. Georgina glanced at Ann, but Ann sat stone-faced, staring straight ahead.

"Do show her in, Kingston, and bring some fresh tea."

Lady Castlereagh was shown in, appearing slightly damp from her travels. The ladies made polite conversation until the tea arrived. Georgina knew Lady Castlereagh would never be so gauche as to ask for her voucher back in front on Kingston. Though, she had to admit, she was rather surprised that the lady would arrive in person to ask for it. It seemed the sort of thing a person might more easily do by post.

Kingston laid the tea and shut the door. As Georgina's mother poured, Lady Castlereagh said, "I know perfectly well I should have waited to call until this blasted rain has stopped, but I felt I wanted to come immediately."

And here it was. Georgina braced herself. Ann gripped the arms of the chair.

"Well?" Lady Castlereagh said, looking from one face to another. "Have you received them?"

"Received what?" Lady Marksley asked.

That was exactly what Georgina wanted to know. Received what?

"My dear," Lady Castlereagh said to Georgina's mother. "The summons. It's the absolute talk of the town."

"I know nothing of a summons," Lady Marksley said. "A summons from whom to what?"

"Ah," Lady Castlereagh said, "your post has been delayed. There can be no doubt of Georgina and Ann receiving them. Now, I wonder if I should ruin the surprise."

Georgina prayed that Lady Castlereagh would, indeed, ruin the surprise. Whatever this mystery was, it had nothing to do with losing her voucher to Almack's. Now that she could relax, she desperately wanted to know what was causing the excitement.

"Do not tease, my dear Lady Castlereagh," Georgina's mother said. "You have me quite intrigued, you must tell me what you speak of."

Lady Castlereagh took her tea and set it down. "All right, I will. It's all too delicious to keep to myself. I shall tell you all I know of it."

Georgina and Ann glanced at each other. Lady Castlereagh began.

"An invitation, or I should say, a summons, has begun arriving for all the best girls." She glanced kindly at Georgina and Ann. "And here, of course, we have two such girls. Now," she continued, "you shall never guess who it is from."

Lady Castlereagh paused, as if they would try to make a guess. Georgina was completely stumped. Was the Prince throwing another ball perhaps?

"It is from the Dowager Countess of Knightsbridge," Lady Castlereagh said.

"Oh my," Georgina's mother said. "I have not seen the dowager these many years."

"Few of us have," Lady Castlereagh answered. "She never comes to town. A gouty leg, I believe. But that is of no import. What is so unusual is what the dowager has to say in this summons. I shall try to repeat it from memory, though you shall have your own soon enough."

Georgina could hardly follow what Lady Castlereagh was saying. The Dowager Countess of Knightsbridge was Lord Greystone's mother.

"It goes like this," Lady Castlereagh said. "As my son is in want of a wife, and as you have been recommended to me, I hereby summon you to Greystone Hall for a week-long house party. You may bring family as a chaperone, though I have arranged to have plentiful ladies with eyes like hawks to do the job. Traveling arrangements will be made for you. I am determined to have a look at you to ensure my son chooses wisely. If you are engaged to be married to someone else, or nearly so, do not come. I will expect you on the 23rd.

Warmly, the Dowager Countess of Knightsbridge.

"That is most extraordinary," Lady Marksley said. "The Dowager was always a bit eccentric. I see she has not changed."

"Absolutely everyone is talking about it," Lady Castlereagh said. "Have you ever heard of anything so diverting? Lady Tennesby says that she heard that some gentleman will be brought in for a ball, but that is only so that there are enough dancing partners to make a ball. The real point is, as the Dowager says, Greystone wants a wife."

"It is an unusual way to go about it," Lady Marksley said. "He must be quite determined."

"Lady Tennesby says that on the last evening, at the end of the ball, Greystone will propose. Assuming he is accepted, and I cannot imagine the girl who would not accept the Earl of Knightsbridge, he shall jump on his horse and ride like the wind to the girl's father. It's all deadly romantic."

Georgina's heart sank. It *was* all deadly romantic, but nothing to do with her. Her poor mother assumed that her own and Ann's summons were delayed in the post. Georgina knew it was not coming. What easier way for Greystone to shame her bad behavior than have her excluded from the summons. And, even if he were not determined to punish her, he would never want to be associated with Edmund.

Her lack of a summons would be noted, Georgina knew. People would speculate that she was engaged or nearly so, or had somehow offended Lord Greystone. It would be just a mercy that no one but Ann would know how far she had gone to offend him. She supposed Miss Stanhope was admiring her summons at that very moment.

Lady Castlereagh left. Despite the rain, she was making a round of calls to see what else was known about the summons and which other girls had received one.

"Quite extraordinary," Lady Marksley said. "Georgi, you've seen Lord Greystone enough times, does he appear to be determined to be married?"

Georgina held her hands together so they would not shake. "I hardly know," she said.

Two days passed with no summons. Two days of long reflection for Georgina. The idea that all those girls, how many she did not know, had been summoned to Greystone Hall. That Lord Greystone would dance with them and talk with them, and finally propose to one of them, gnawed at her insides.

At first, she had attributed that gnawing feeling to the embarrassment she would suffer when it was known that she had not received a summons. There she would be, for all to see, wandering around London while other girls had flocked to Hampshire. There she would be, under her mother's penetrating gaze, as Lady Marksley pressed her for what she had done to offend the man.

Soon though, she began to realize the gnawing feeling was something else entirely. Now that she understood Greystone's true character, she had slowly allowed herself to like him. She had allowed herself to believe that Ann was right – sooner or later there would be an opportunity to apologize so they might begin again.

She had been wrong to allow herself to believe they might begin again. There would be no starting over with Lord Greystone. Georgina laughed bitterly. Of course she had been wrong. What hadn't she been wrong about?

Lady Marksley was truly beginning to fret on the third day. Kingston brought in the post and Georgina steeled herself for another round of disappointment from her mother.

Kingstone held out the tray.

"Finally," her mother said.

Georgina looked up.

"One for you," she said, handing Georgina a letter. "One for Ann, and one for myself."

Georgina eyed the letter in her hands. It was indeed from the Dowager Countess of Knightsbridge. Hope bubbled up, quickly replaced by fear. Just because she had received a letter, did not mean she had received a summons. For all she knew, the Dowager wrote to tell Georgina that her son had expressly asked that she not be invited.

Lady Marksley had already opened her letter. "The Dowager Countess says I may come if I like, though it is not necessary. Lady Tennesby and Lady Worthington will act as chaperones. Well, it would be interesting enough to see how you get on Georgina, but I may well forgo it. My bones are just recovering from the trip to town and I trust Lady Tennesby to keep you out of any mischief."

Her mother may come if she likes. Surely that meant that what she held in her hands was a summons. Georgina ripped open the letter. There it was. The glorious summons, with 'my son is in want of a wife' and all. Somehow, Lord Greystone would not punish her. Perhaps he understood from her outburst that she had not had all the facts. No matter, he had not blackballed her. She would go. When she got there, she would look for an opportunity to apologize. Perhaps she and Lord Greystone really could begin again.

Georgina smiled. Miss Stanhope would not be happy to see her.

Chapter Eleven

Georgina, Ann and her mother spent a week buying and arranging and deciding what to pack for the house party at Greystone Hall. News began to circulate around the ton. Who was going? Who was not? Rumor had it that Lord Greystone had left town. No one was sure exactly when he had gone, but all were sure he was at his estate readying for the house party.

Ann surveyed Georgina's bedroom, which was awash in gowns and gloves and hats and undergarments. "You shall never get all this packed, Georgina."

Georgina laughed. "I never should," she said. "But Jemma will. She is a master magician at packing."

Jemma blushed and continued sorting a pile of ribbons.

"Now Ann," Georgina said, "it occurs to me that your lady's maid is a terrible traveler. You remember the ride to town? She was…indisposed. Why not leave her here? I'm sure she would be grateful and Jemma is clever enough to care for us both. I will even give Jemma a crown at the end of it to compensate the extra work."

"Oh," Ann said. "You are right about Fleur. I can tell already she is dreading the trip. But I would not like to overburden Jemma."

Jemma put down her pile of ribbons. "Two crowns," she said. She eyed Ann's hair. "And I'll need extra time with the curling tongs."

"Where on earth did I get such a cheeky maid?" Georgina asked, laughing.

"She is only a truth-teller," Ann said ruefully as she patted her hair. "She is quite right about the extra time."

"No matter," Georgina said gaily. "We shall work it out somehow and Jemma will have her two crowns."

Jemma smiled and continued on with her ribbons.

"Georgina," Ann said, "you are in better spirits than I have seen you in many weeks. I was right, was I not? You do like Lord Greystone?"

Georgina was silent for a moment. Then she said, "In truth, you were right. Though it took some thinking on my part. I was so disposed to hate him! But, that was my silly pride and I had no idea what Edmund had done. Or what Greystone had done for Edmund and, in turn, for us."

Georgina also could not help reflecting on the fact that Greystone had shown real concern for the poor souls suffering from fever. He had shown mercy, to both Edmund and herself as well. He had the sort of character that she had thought Edmund had, under all the smiles and jokes. How little a person's demeanor told a person what lay underneath! Edmund's laughter masked a selfish and unprincipled character, while Lord Greystone's seriousness masked a man who worked to help those less fortunate then himself and, if the summons was anything to go by, was not inclined to hold a grudge.

Georgina and Ann spoke often of what Edmund had done, without noting any of the specifics. It would be impossible that the staff remain unaware that he had done something serious, the staff were like falcons – their vision was sharp and they missed nothing. However, Georgina and Ann were determined that the staff should never know what in particular Edmund had done. For all his faults, he would still be the next Viscount. The staff might forgive him a dalliance or a debt, but they would never respect a gentleman who had cheated at cards.

Ann had written to Edmund and told him that she had allowed Georgina to read his letter. He was to give up all hopes of a match. Edmund had not replied and Ann feared he was very angry with her, but she was convinced that it had to be done. She would not let Edmund carry on that foolishness any longer.

The awaited day came and Georgina peered out the window all morning, waiting for the carriage. It was not to come until ten to begin the two-day journey to Greystone Hall. Lady Marksley had received a flurry of correspondence prior to the day. It appeared that Georgina and Ann would be escorted by Lady Tennesby and her tallest footmen, and they would stay at an inn to break the journey. Georgina had never in her life stayed overnight at an inn and was looking forward to the adventure, despite her mother saying it was generally unremarkable, except to be uncomfortable.

Georgina breathed in the fresh morning air. It was a fine day to begin a journey. London had left behind the series of spring storms that had so vexed everyone. Finally, she heard the clip-clop of horse's hooves coming into the courtyard.

Kingston helped Lady Tennesby down from a smart-looking coach as another of the same size pulled up behind. Georgina shut the window and raced down the stairs.

After Lady Tennesby was greeted, the chaos of packing ensued. There were two carriages, one for Lady Tennesby, Ann and Georgina and another for the lady's maids and the luggage. Fleur had been grateful to be excused from the journey and she cheerfully helped Jemma and Lady Tennesby's maid arrange boxes of every description. After an hour of frenzied rearranging and checking, everything was packed, goodbyes were said and Georgina peered out the window and waved at her mother as the carriage left Berkeley Square. Her adventure had begun.

Georgina felt jittery in the carriage, not only to be on her way to Greystone Hall, but to be under such close scrutiny of Lady Tennesby. Lady Tennesby was a great friend of her mother's and Georgina felt that of all the ladies she knew her best. However, it was one thing to entertain with tea for a half hour and another to be confined to a carriage for the better part of two days. Georgina worried that she would not be able to survive that many hours without saying something she should not.

Fortunately, calm and sensible Ann was there to allay her nerves. Lady Tennesby was in a jolly mood and they spoke at length about Greystone Hall, which she had visited many times as she was childhood friends with the dowager. She said the joke was that it was called Greystone Hall and not Greystone Castle. The building was enormous and built in the Baroque style. It was situated at a high elevation and sported magnificent formal gardens and a rose garden and had a lake on either side of the house. The interior was tastefully done and Lady Tennesby particularly approved of the drawing room, being done up in turquoise.

"You will be quite charmed by it, girls," Lady Tennesby said. "As I am charmed by the Dowager Countess' scheme. When she requested I compose a list of suitable girls, you two were the first I thought of."

Georgina's heart skipped a beat. "But," she stammered, "*you* devised the list? I would have thought that…"

"That the Dowager Countess was the author?" Lady Tennesby asked. "Yes, I did allow your mother to think it, as the Dowager insisted on complete secrecy. It would have been quite impossible though, the lady hasn't been to town for years."

"I believe what Georgina meant," Ann said quietly, her face full of alarm, "is that it was Lord Greystone's list."

"Lord Greystone? Certainly not," Lady Tennesby said. "As I understand it, the Dowager had to prevail upon him to agree to the whole idea. She feels his bachelor days should have been over last year and insists he get on with it."

Lady Tennesby chose the girls! Why had she been so sure Greystone himself made the list? Georgina felt frozen in her seat. She had thought the summons indicated that he would not be unhappy to see her. As it was, she was about to become a very unwelcome guest.

She willed the carriage to turn around and go back to Berkeley Square, but it rolled ever forward. How could she face him? She would seem a shameless schemer, arriving where she knew perfectly well she was not wanted.

Lady Tennesby had dozed off. Georgina caught Ann's eye. If the look on her cousin's face was anything to go by, this would be dreadful indeed. Somehow she must get through the visit without anyone noticing how much she was not welcome.

Why had she allowed herself to like him? She really was so foolhardy. Georgina felt that from now on, whenever she had an idea or opinion, she would immediately adopt the opposite stance as it was bound to be right.

The hours passed by slowly and Georgina thought of various ways she might escape the house party. She might feign an illness, or pretend to receive post with sad news about a relation that required her to return to her family immediately. Either idea would have been suitable, if only Lady Tennesby had not been there. The lady was too close to her mother for Georgina to be able to claim a dead relation. Pretending an illness had its own risks. In Hampshire, she was closer to Marksley Manor than she was to London and might very well be sent home for the rest of the season to recover. And then there was her inability to feign an illness, she had tried it as a child and always been remarkably unsuccessful. She did not have the sort of pale looks that did so well at looking sickly, she was too robustly healthy-looking.

Late in the afternoon, the carriage pulled into the Grantsby Arms. It was a large and respectable-looking place with a busy courtyard and rooms on the second floor. Georgina and Ann were shown to a room that could only be accessed by passing through Lady Tennesby's room. Georgina thought her mother correct in placing her faith in Lady Tennesby. No harm could come to them without the perpetrator getting by Lady Tennesby and her maid first.

As the door shut, Georgina grabbed Ann's arms and whispered, "What shall I do? He shall be furious to see me in his own house!"

"You do not know that," Ann said softly, though the look on her face said quite plainly that she thought the same.

"Do not try to comfort me, Ann," Georgina said. "You know as well as I do that Greystone has no idea I am about to walk through his door and he will not be happy to see me."

"And not happy to see me either," Ann said. "After all, Edmund is my brother."

"Oh, dear Ann, how thoughtless of me to forget your own discomfort."

"Now, there," Ann said, patting Georgina's arm, "there's nothing to be done about it but hold our heads high."

"I hardly know how I will do it," Georgina said. "You are always so calm, but I feel likely to burst into tears in the drawing room."

"You will do no such thing," Ann said sternly. "We are not in the wrong. We received a summons, and we have answered it. We have no responsibility for who did or did not write this ridiculous list."

Georgina took heart from Ann's words. Ann was right, how were they to know who wrote the list of girls? They had received a summons and very politely answered it and that was all. If Greystone wanted to make a fuss, then that would be just his own bad manners.

Georgina went down to dinner in better spirits. The waiter showed she and Ann and Lady Tennesby to a private room. Georgina had not seen any other girls and speculated that they must all be put up at different inns somewhere near the half-way mark to Greystone Hall.

She was entranced with the menu. Georgina had never ordered off of a menu in her life. How convenient that each person could eat what they liked. Someday, when she was married and well-established and could afford to bend the rules, she would host a dinner party replete with a menu. It would be a true novelty.

The waiter interrupted her thoughts. "Lord Greystone has instructed," he said with a serious air, "that you are his guests and are to order what you like best. He has taken the liberty of delivering wine from his own cellar."

The waiter uncorked the wine, filled their glasses and bowed himself from the room.

"Greystone is a charming host," Lady Tennesby said, sipping her wine. She looked at Georgina and said, "No doubt we shall be a gay party this coming week."

Georgina had every doubt of it, though she could hardly say so to Lady Tennseby. Thinking to change the subject, Georgina said, "Can you tell us of the Dowager Countess?"

"Ah, yes," Lady Tennesby said. "I have known the Dowager since she was a girl. She was headstrong then, and remains so. When she has opinions, and she often does, she is not afraid to say them. She is sharp-witted and nothing much will get past her notice. She is fond of her children, but never overly indulgent."

Fond of her children, but not overly indulgent. Georgina suspected that had gone a great length to form Greystone's character. If she were honest, knowing what she did of Edmund, Ann's parents might have used a firmer hand on him to good effect.

"I suspect," Lady Tennesby continued, "knowing her as I do, that she will not be impressed with any false feminine wiles. Have a care, girls, if you seek to gain the approval of the Dowager Countess. Leave any thought of silliness behind. I understand Sir Halford refers to it as 'fan waving and swooning.' That will not endear you to her at all."

Georgina thought fan waving and swooning was the least of her problems. Her real difficulty would be not attracting the notice of this formidable creature. If she did, the Dowager was sure to notice that Greystone actively disliked her.

Georgina tossed and turned throughout the night. The mattress was lumpy, Jemma snored like thunder in the cot next to her bed and she could not rid herself of the dread of the next day's arrival to Greystone Hall.

The morning dawned bright and fine, the weather seemed to mock Georgina's dark mood. She had hoped to delay their departure as long as possible. The last thing she could imagine was being the first to arrive. She rather hoped to slip in unnoticed, the drawing room already busy with the chatter of the other girls. No matter, Lady Tennesby hustled them through breakfast and before she knew it they were barreling down the post road.

Ann did her best to entertain Lady Tennesby and occasionally kicked Georgina's leg to remind her to say something. Georgina would comment on the view and then sink back into feeling as if she were on the way to her own hanging.

Lady Tennesby had already said, "We're nearly there," twice, so Georgina could only believe that they were, in fact, nearly there. Why did a carriage wheel never break when it would be convenient? Where were the highwaymen that could waylay them and delay their arrival? It seemed to Georgina that when a person desired to reach their destination quickly, all manner of mishaps occurred. Yet when a person was in no such hurry, everything went smoothly along.

"There are the gates," Lady Tennesby said.

Georgina peeked out the window. Iron gates twice the height of a man were ensconced in a massive stone archway. Beyond, she could see a lane that crested a hill and disappeared. Perhaps the road to the house was miles long, and would afford some extra time.

"The house is just over that crest," Lady Tennesby said.

Georgina sighed.

A stooped old man emerged from the carriage house and swung the gates open. Georgina had a strong desire to lean out the window and call, 'We are not the first to arrive, are we? Tell me we are not!' Instead, she folded her hands together to steady them.

Ann gave her a look that Georgina knew was meant to say, 'chin up.' She supposed there was nothing else to do but that.

The carriage drove over the crest of the hill. Georgina's first view of Greystone Hall took her breath away. It was a pale stone house of massive proportions. In its center rose a gold-plated dome, with the wings of the house on either side. Its roofs were decorated with intricate stone carvings. Georgina had never seen anything like it outside of her father's books on French architecture.

The staff filed out of the large front doors and formed two neat rows on either side of the entrance. Georgina noticed that instead of a step up to the door, there was a gently sloping ramp. As the carriage came to a stop, she saw why. The Dowager Countess was wheeled out in a chair to greet them.

Georgina had known the Dowager suffered from rheumatism or gout or some such malady, but had not known she was confined to a chair. Poor woman!

Georgina noted the sharp eyes on the dowager and thought that though her legs might be crippled, her mind certainly was not. She was a petite woman with powdered curls swept up in an elegant arrangement. A velvet shawl was draped gracefully around her shoulders to protect her from the chill country air.

The first footman opened the carriage door and the butler helped Lady Tennesby down. She greeted the Dowager with a kiss on the cheek. "Lovely to see you, Lydia," she said.

"You should come to Greystone Hall more than twice a year," the Dowager said. "You could hardly avoid seeing me then."

Lady Tennesby laughed. "You have not changed one bit."

"I suppose not at my age," the Dowager said. "Who have you brought me?"

Ann was already out of the carriage and Georgina was being helped down. They both curtsied deeply as Lady Tennesby said, "Miss Georgina Marksley, she's Katherine Marksley's girl. And Ann Carrington, daughter of Sir Carrington."

"Welcome girls," the Dowager said in a kinder, softer voice. "You two look as if you've seen a dragon. Come here, I do not bite."

Georgina and Ann approached and the Dowager took a closer look at them. She especially stared at Georgina. "I used to know Lady Marksley when I was still in the habit of visiting town," she said. "Charming woman."

Georgina bowed her head and said, "My mother remembers you fondly, ma'am."

"Give her my regards," the Dowager said. "Now, we cannot spend the day outdoors. Smith, wheel me in."

Smith, a tall footman who seemed to be well-accustomed to wheeling the dowager in her chair, turned the lady and wheeled her up the ramp. The ramp was promptly removed by two of the lower footman to reveal stone steps. Ann and Georgina followed Lady Tennesby inside.

Georgina hadn't been able to surmise if there were other girls arrived yet and entered the hall with trepidation, as if Lord Greystone would by laying in wait and ready to pounce.

Mercifully, he was nowhere to be seen. Georgina gazed around the great hall, it was truly remarkable. The ceiling height must have been well over eighty feet, capped off by an exquisite dome. The furnishings were luxurious and covered with brocades in rich colors. Fine artwork hung on the walls and the floor was polished pink marble. A grand staircase curved up to the higher floor.

The Dowager Countess raised one hand in the air and made a circle. Smith spun her around to face her guests. "Mrs. Claydon is my housekeeper, she will escort you to your rooms. Tea at three, be down for dinner at six-thirty, we dine at seven. You will find a schedule in your room."

She waved her hand in the air again and Smith pushed her down the hall and into one of the galleries.

Mrs. Claydon, an efficient middle-aged woman, hustled them up the stairs to their rooms. As they went, she explained that all the girls were to be in the east wing with Lady Tennesby and Lady Worthington as chaperones. The family and the gentleman guests would be in the west. Georgina thought at least there would be no danger of encountering Lord Greystone in the hall.

"If I may ask, who are the gentleman guests, Lady Tennesby?" Ann asked as they ascended the stairs.

Clever Ann. Georgina had not even thought to inquire, though if there were some that she knew that might go a long way in keeping herself out of Lord Greystone's way.

"I haven't the faintest idea," Lady Tennesby said. "Friends of Lord Greystone's, I presume."

Mrs. Claydon showed Georgina and Ann to their rooms. Georgina was awed by the size of her bedchamber. The massive bed, covered in a blue velvet counterpane with crisp lawn sheets underneath, was dwarfed by the size of the space. The walls were covered in a blue paper and a braided silk bell-pull hung next to the bed to call for Jemma in the morning. Her luggage had already been brought up.

Georgina ran to the windows. They reached floor to ceiling and were covered with heavy brocade drapes. She pulled one back and her breath caught at the view. Formal gardens with neatly clipped box hedges stretched out below her. Beyond the gardens, acres of green lawn covered the gently sloping land, ending at the tree line of an oak wood. She could just glimpse the blue of the lakes on either side of the house.

Georgina heard a gentle tap on the door and Jemma entered.

"How do you find things downstairs?" Georgina asked. She knew from visiting various relations that for Jemma the key to enjoying the trip was her reception from the house's staff, the sleeping accommodations and the food.

"They're a friendly bunch," Jemma said. "The Dowager runs things tight, but she's liberal with dinner and I'm only sharing a bedchamber with Lady Tennesby's maid."

"That sounds promising," Georgina said. "I am glad you shall find yourself well-rested, as you will no doubt earn your two crowns running from room to room."

"No running necessary," Jemma said, tapping on a door that Georgina had assumed led to a closet.

"Enter," Ann said from the other room.

Georgina poked her head through the doorway. "Our rooms are connected! How clever." In truth, Georgina was happy about the easy access to Ann's room for more than cleverness. She felt she had no one to rely on but Ann and it was comforting to know she could find her whenever necessary without having to encounter someone in the hall.

Jemma was busy unpacking Georgina's cases. Georgina stepped into Ann's room. It was just as glorious as Georgina's bedchamber, though done up in pale pink.

"This would be so pleasant," Georgina said, "if the circumstances were not so unpleasant."

"Perhaps it will be easier than you imagine," Ann said. She had picked up a piece of vellum that lay on the night table. "The schedule. Apparently we will dine with the gentleman this evening, but will not see them afterward. Unless you are seated next to Lord Greystone at dinner, there may be no opportunity to say anything to him at all."

That was odd. Georgina had never gone to a dinner that did not follow the same strict guidelines – walk in to dinner, afterward the ladies would retire to the drawing room, then the gentleman would join them after port. She took the schedule from Ann's hand.

The entry for the day said, 'Dinner at seven, after which the ladies will gather in the drawing room to become better acquainted with the Dowager Countess of Knightsbridge. The gentlemen will play billiards or otherwise occupy the evening on their own.'

"I may be reprieved for today, then," Georgina said. "Now I only need worry about the other five days."

"I like the Dowager Countess very much," Ann said.

"I, as well," Georgina said. She meant it, too. She felt that familiar wave of regret wash over her. The 'if only.' If only she had watched her tongue, she might have found herself with a real reason to be at Greystone Hall. If only she had not assumed she knew everything there was to know, she might be looking on this week as an exciting adventure. As it was, she was trying to figure out how to hide from Lord Greystone for an entire week in his own house.

Georgina heard giggling in the hall. It faded away as the giggler moved past. She and Ann would not be the only girls here for tea, that was a comfort anyway.

Jemma strode into the room and began on Ann's cases. Georgina heard a carriage rumbling over the gravel outside. She peeked out of Ann's window. Lady Worthington was being greeted by the Dowager. As Georgina continued to view the scene, she saw her and Ann's friend, Miss Lennox. Then Miss Hargrave. As she was about to let the drape fall, she saw one more head emerging from the carriage. A head full of blond curls. Miss Stanhope.

Georgina sighed. She had no doubt that by the end of the week, Lord Greystone and Miss Stanhope would be engaged.

Jemma had laid out Georgina's tea dress. It was time to prepare to go down.

The drawing room was as Lady Tennesby described, charmingly done. The walls were covered with turquoise patterned paper and the chairs done to match. The carpet was a rich rose and the wainscoting done in white with gold leaf. A large crystal chandelier hung in the center of the room.

Lady Tennesby poured tea, surrounded by the Misses Stanhope, Hargrave and Lennox.

Georgina was relieved to see that the Dowager had not yet made an appearance. As much as she liked the woman, she felt it wise to keep her distance, lest she be asked her history with Lord Greystone. She was not sure how she might accomplish avoiding her this evening, since the stated point of it was to become better acquainted with the dowager, but she would try.

Ann took her arm and led her forward. "Ah, Miss Marksley and Miss Carrington," Lady Tennesby said. She smiled at Georgina, seeming to notice her nervousness. "Relax, my dear," she said. "We shall be quite a cozy group for tea. The Dowager will not make an appearance until dinner."

Georgina smiled gratefully at Lady Tennesby, who handed her a cup of tea. Lady Tennesby was clearly under the impression that Georgina was all nerves because she hoped to win over the Dowager.

Ann and Georgina greeted the other girls, with an especially warm greeting to their friend Miss Lennox.

"This is most extraordinary," Miss Lennox said as they sat together. "I hardly know how we all got here. My mother and father were initially quite alarmed about the whole thing, but Lady Tennesby allayed their fears. They trust her implicitly."

"As does my mother," Georgina said. "Though as you say, the situation is quite extraordinary."

"I really feel," Miss Lennox said, "that Lord Greystone must have his eye on someone, and I am certain it is not me."

Ann nodded. "I feel quite the same."

"As do I," Georgina said, though she felt that she had reason to be even more confident of it then Ann and Miss Lennox.

"I do not know, Georgina," Miss Lennox said. "You're very fetching-looking. You and Miss Stanhope are the beauties of the season."

Georgina blushed. At the mention of Miss Stanhope, she stole a look across the room. Miss Stanhope was conversing with Lady Tennesby on some amusing subject. Of course, she would be. She had no doubt determined to conquer Lady Tennesby, Lady Worthington and the Dowager, thereby securing Lord Greystone.

Georgina noticed that Miss Hastings-Bass had arrived. Everyone knew that this was her third season. She curtsied and smiled at Lady Tennesby, but Georgina thought there was a look of quiet desperation on her face. She could only imagine the pressure the poor girl was under from her parents. Miss Hastings-Bass was probably under strict orders to hook and reel in the Earl of Knightsbridge. Poor girl! How could she return home and tell her mother that it had been Miss Stanhope all along?

Georgina wondered if she would be in the same position two years from now. She had thought picking out a husband would be the easiest thing in the world. Now she saw that the marriage mart was fraught with peril and a girl was lucky to get out unscathed.

She watched Ann and Miss Lennox as they discussed the books they had read recently. Again, she envied Ann's steady regard for Sir Langston.

Georgina almost felt as if she were in a dream, or in some way watching from outside herself. The tall and auburn-haired Miss Smith had arrived, shortly followed by Miss Cavendish and Miss Templeton, who repaired to their own quiet corner as always. Perhaps Greystone would not choose Miss Stanhope after all, perhaps he would choose Miss Cavendish or Miss Templeton. They were just as reserved and serious as he was. Georgina smiled as she remembered how Ann had scolded her for referring to them as the "Colicky Cousins."

Georgina woke from her reverie in time to hear Lady Tennesby say to the room, "I shall see you at dinner."

Jemma fussed with Georgina's gown, a lilac satin that her mother had made specially for the trip. She had to admit, despite her penchant for darker colors, the lilac set off her looks nicely.

Jemma curled the last curl as the dinner gong was rung. There was no delaying now. She must go down to the drawing room and spend a half hour avoiding Lord Greystone and the Dowager, and then pray she was not seated near him at dinner. The worst part, she knew, was seeing the look on his face when he saw that she was to be one of the party. Had Lady Tennesby told him who she had put on the list? She thought not, as the housekeeper had not arrived and offered to pack Georgina's bags and put her in a coach.

Would anything that dreadful happen? No, really she did not think so. Greystone was far too reserved to cause a scene. The worst that would happen was that it would be apparent to all that he held her in no regard.

"Are you ready, Georgina?"

Ann had come through the connecting door. She was beautifully dressed in a pale green silk and Jemma had done a remarkable job of creating curls.

"You look lovely," Georgina said.

"Thank you, as do you. Now, enough compliments." Ann took Georgina's hand and said, "It's time to march ourselves into the lion's den."

The drawing room was crowded by the time Ann and Georgina entered. The rest of the girls were already there, along with Lady Tennesby, Lady Worthington and the Dowager. The men had also come down, and Georgina was thankful that she recognized them all. There was Lord Tansby of the fish eyes, Mr. Ledbridge - a poor second son of an Earl, Lord Vanderman - just recently an Earl and Sir Lewis – only a Baronet, but invited to all the best places because of his jolly temperament.

So these were Lord Greystone's friends? Georgina would not have thought it, as she knew them all to be friendly and outgoing.

Georgina was relieved to see that Lord Greystone himself had not made an appearance. Georgina quickly moved to a group comprised of Lord Tansby, Miss Smith and Miss Hargrave to hide herself in the crowd.

A footman handed her a glass of wine and she sipped it to steady her nerves.

"Ah," the Dowager said loudly, "there's my son."

Georgina froze and slowly turned to the door.

Lord Greystone stood in the doorway, his broad shoulders nearly filling the space. His light hair was brushed back and he was tan, as if he had been out riding for many hours. Georgina thought the tan particularly set off his grey eyes.

Greystone searched the room, his gaze settling on Georgina. He did not look angry, rather, he looked unaccountably pleased.

He moved toward her, until Miss Stanhope put herself in his way.

Could it be possible? After everything she had said, he was not furious? Georgina glanced at Ann. She could tell by her cousin's smile that Ann had noted it too. If it were so, then the man really was inscrutable. If it were so, they might be able to begin again.

Georgina watched his manner with Miss Stanhope closely, until she saw him look over her blond curls at Georgina. Before she could ponder it any further, Mr. Ledbridge held out his arm to take her to dinner. She could see Ann being steered out by Lord Tansby. Poor Tansby, he had no idea how devoted Ann was to Sir Langston.

Miss Stanhope very brazenly put her arm out for Lord Greystone. He looked resigned as he took it.

Through the courses at dinner, Georgina did her best to entertain Mr. Ledbridge on her right, and Miss Cavendish on her left. It was an odd seating arrangement, as there were nine girls present and only five gentlemen, the result being some of the girls were left without a dinner partner. Mr. Ledbridge was fairly easy to amuse, Miss Cavendish was another matter. The girl was reserved to the point of mute.

When she thought she might go unnoticed, Georgina stole glances at Greystone at the head of the table. Miss Stanhope was clearly working hard to amuse. Georgina felt it would be kind to let the girl know that Lord Greystone did not get amused. Miss Stanhope would do better to pursue a more serious conversation.

Georgina smiled to herself. Did she really think she knew him better than all others? Probably not, but she did think she was beginning to understand his character. She liked his character very much.

How strange life was, changing so quickly, even in the smallest of things. An hour ago she had prayed she would not be seated next to Greystone and now she was heartily sorry that she was not. She must always remember, from all she had learned over the past months, that her opinion on any particular matter was ever subject to change.

The dinner ended and the ladies retired to the drawing room. Before she had known that Greystone would not hate that she was there, she had intended to do everything she could to avoid speaking with the Dowager. Now, she looked forward to it.

"Girls," the Dowager said, after the footman had wheeled her in front of the fire, "I am not one to mince words, as you most likely gathered when you received my note. I am also not one to enjoy the traditional simpering female. So please, when you speak with me, simply be yourself and not some cake-baked version of what you think an elegant female should be."

Georgina covered her mouth to hide a smile. Some of the other girls looked less amused and positively nervous. After all, they had spent the past years being trained to be a cake-baked elegant female. Georgina was sure that some of the girls did not quite understand what the Dowager wanted, but were convinced she could not mean they be their natural selves. Who in the world would do that in society?

"I'm quite serious about finding a wife for my son," the Dowager continued. "I also know exactly what I am looking for and will see through any artifice, so do not even attempt it. I shall speak to you privately, one by one. While I am speaking to one of you, the rest may go to the other side of the drawing room and amuse yourself with cards or the piano."

The Dowager pointed to Ann and said, "You, Miss Carrington, I will see you first."

As Georgina walked to the other side of the room with the rest of the girls, she heard the Dowager say, "Hair straight as a pin. I've got the same problem myself. Your maid is to be commended."

Georgina giggled to herself. She would tell Jemma of the compliment as she readied for bed. Jemma would quite enjoy it and no doubt repeat it endlessly to the entire Marksley staff.

"Miss Marksley," Miss Stanhope said. Georgina thought it sounded less like a greeting and more like an inquiry as to why she was there.

She curtsied and said, "Miss Stanhope."

"You seem to pop up everywhere," Miss Stanhope said, again in a tone that indicated that she did not think it was an admirable quality.

"Yes, indeed," Georgina said. "My old governess would say I'm much like a bad penny, always turning up unexpectedly."

Miss Stanhope turned and flounced to the piano. Georgina stole a look at the other side of the drawing room. The Dowager and Ann were deep in conversation. Whatever Ann was saying to the lady, she was saying it in earnest.

The Dowager nodded and patted her hand. After another fifteen minutes, Ann rose and joined Georgina. Miss Stanhope was called to the Dowager.

"We have much to talk about," Ann said.

Georgina nodded. They stole away to a quiet corner. Georgina could not contain herself. "Well?" she said. "Did you note that Lord Greystone did not throw me out on my ear?"

"I did," Ann said, smiling at her. "In truth, Georgina, he often looked at you at dinner. I think Miss Stanhope was quite put out."

"I am just so relieved," Georgina said. "Now I will not have to prowl around the house like a ghost, hoping to go unseen."

"Is that all?" Ann asked.

"No," Georgina admitted. "You know perfectly well that is not all. But, one victory at a time. I am just glad it appears we may begin again and that may very well be all there is. The blond Miss Stanhope has every chance of success."

Ann did not look convinced, but Georgina could not bear talking of it any further. "Tell me of your talk with the Dowager."

Ann colored, then she said, "I like her more than ever, but I will warn you that she was not in jest when she directed us to be our real selves. She cut through my defenses in an instant and I found myself revealing things to her that I never…" Ann trailed off.

"She's discovered Sir Langston, that is it, is it not?"

"Yes," Ann whispered. "Though I very much do not like to talk about it since there is no formal understanding between us. It seems unlucky somehow and I told her so. She patted my hand and said, 'I understand perfectly. Many a slip between the cup and the lip.' Then she told me I was welcome to stay the week though, based on my feelings, I was a thoroughly unsuitable match for her son."

"Extraordinary," Georgina said.

"Yes," Ann answered. "Yes, she is."

Miss Stanhope returned to the group of girls. She looked unhappy and Georgina could only wonder what the Dowager had managed to pry out of her. She stomped over to Georgina and Ann and said, "Miss Marksley? The Dowager will see you."

Georgina smiled ruefully. Now she could wonder what the Dowager was about to pry out of herself. No matter, she thought, she would heed the lady's advice and just be herself, for good or ill.

She sat down across from the Dowager. The fire was high and Georgina felt her cheeks warm from the heat.

The Dowager poured her a cup of tea and said, "Miss Marksley, tell me of your temperament, warts and all."

Georgina was startled. She took this to mean that the Dowager would like to know her faults. She had not been in the habit of advertising her less than perfect qualities, but she could see from the Dowager's sharp eyes that there was no use prevaricating.

"Well," Georgina said. "I am high-spirited. I used to think it a very good quality, but over the past few months I have seen that it can also be problematic. I am kind to my servants and my father's tenants, but probably give my maid far too much leeway. And too much money, too."

Rather than looking shocked, the Dowager looked amused.

"And worst of all, I am too quick to judge. I often think I know a person's character instantly, and then find out later that I was quite mistaken. In short, ma'am, I began this first season with all the confidence in the world and I will end it very much less sure of myself."

The Dowager nodded. "I am certain you think this predicament particular to you, and yet it is not. You are simply moving from a girl to a woman. Bravo to you, Miss Marksley. Some females never do and leave life just as silly as they came into it."

Georgina could feel her cheeks flaming ever pinker. She also felt a profound sense of relief. She had bared all and there was nothing to hide.

"Now, you thought that a highly personal question, but it will pale in comparison to what I will ask you now," the Dowager said. "How do you feel about my son?"

Georgina felt as though the ground shook beneath her feet. How could the Dowager ask a girl to reveal her feelings toward a man she was not yet engaged to? It was unheard of. No girl would express any outward interest at all until a proposal had been made, lest she find herself guilty of disappointed hopes and a complete laughingstock.

"I am aware of the indelicacy of the question, Miss Marksley. But I ask it anyway, and assure you that your feelings will stay in confidence. I am prying the same information out of each and every one of you and, as there are nine of you, eight must return to London without an engagement. I simply must know your heart."

So this was how the Dowager had gotten Ann to speak of Sir Langston. Georgina could not see any way to answer the question, other than complete honesty. She could see that the Dowager was a skilled interrogator and would not settle for anything less. Georgina only hoped the Dowager would look on her as kindly as she was now after she had heard all.

Georgina took a deep breath and said, "In truth, Lord Greystone and I met under unfortunate circumstances to do with my cousin. I blamed your son for something he was not responsible for, and worse, told him about it in no uncertain terms. I thought he had decided to forgive me when I received your summons, and then when I discovered that Lady Tennesby wrote the list, was rather terrified of my reception."

"That's all well and good, my girl," the Dowager said, waving her off. "But do you love him?"

Georgina sat back in stunned silence. She had gone back and forth on her feelings for Greystone and had comforted herself that they might begin again, but she had avoided examining her feelings too closely. She had not allowed herself to think of it in such definite terms. Now it was unavoidable. Did she or did she not?

"Yes," she said quietly.

"Very good," the Dowager said. "Let us just hope you are not one of the heartbroken, crying your way back to London." The Dowager chuckled. "What a picture that paints, eh? Though no doubt there will be tears in somebody's carriage. Now, send Miss Cavendish. It would also please me if you played on the pianoforte. I fear Miss Stanhope has the ears of a bat, or wishes she did."

Georgina left the Dowager in a daze. She vaguely noticed what the Dowager had meant by Miss Stanhope's bat ears. The girl was sitting as close as she reasonably could to the Dowager, no doubt trying to hear what was said.

She sat at the pianoforte and began to play. Ann stood next to her and said, "Well, what did the Dowager manage to pry out of you?"

"Everything," Georgina said. "Absolutely everything.

"

Chapter Twelve

Georgina woke as Jemma pulled back the draperies. It was a fine day, the sun already burning away the morning mist. "Open the window, Jemma, do," Georgina said. She lay in bed, letting the cool spring air wash over her. The breeze felt brand new. She felt brand new. Somehow, unburdening herself to the Dowager had taken a heavy weight off of her mind. Come what may, she loved Lord Greystone. She knew that now. Her heart might get broken, in all likelihood it would, but she no longer had to hide from herself. She realized that was what she had been doing. Hiding from her own feelings.

Georgina rolled over and picked up the schedule. After breakfast, the girls were given the option of staying in and occupying themselves or going out in the carriage to watch the gentleman fish.

"Jemma," she said, leaping out of bed. "I shall be going fishing this morning."

The gentlemen had left earlier in the morning to fish a stocked stream a half mile from the house. Georgina, and the Misses Hargrave, Smith, Hastings-Bass and, of course, Miss Stanhope had elected to go out in the carriage. Georgina had done her best to prevail upon Ann, but Ann was resolute. She would stay in and enjoy the company of Miss Lennox. Miss Cavendish and Miss Templeton would also stay behind, no doubt staring glumly at each other, as was their habit.

Lady Tennesby would act as chaperone. The Dowager Countess would not be seen until afternoon tea.

The morning was glorious and Georgina would have thoroughly enjoyed the carriage ride were if not for the sour looks of Miss Stanhope. Lady Tennesby put it to an end when she said to Miss Stanhope, "Whatever is the matter? You look as if your breakfast did not agree with you."

They arrived at the stream. Lord Greystone stood at water's edge. He had removed his jacket and rolled up his sleeves. Georgina could see the powerful muscles in his forearms flex as he cast his line. Lord Tansby struggled to untangle his line from Mr. Ledbridge's.

The footmen jumped down from the carriage and helped the ladies down. The carriage that had followed was filled with chairs. The footmen placed them at the top of the slope that led down to water's edge.

Georgina sat down and was handed a lemonade. The Dowager Countess, she noticed, saw to her guests very nicely.

The fishing went on for another hour. Georgina smiled. It appeared to her that each man was deadly serious and she felt sorry for any fish that might get in their way. Both Lord Greystone and Lord Tansby had caught fat trout, while Mr. Ledbridge was struggling to catch up with them.

Lord Greystone laid down his pole and walked up the slope. He stopped at Georgina's chair. "Do you like fishing, Miss Marksley?"

These were the first words Greystone had spoken to her since she arrived and they sounded wonderful. There was no hint of recrimination. It appeared she had been thoroughly forgiven.

"I suspect I would quite like fishing," she answered, "but I have never had the chance to try. My father does not have a suitable stream to stock on the estate."

"I would be happy to show you," Greystone said.

"Now?"

"Yes. I did think now," Greystone said, drily. "As we happen to be by a well-stocked stream and conveniently find ourselves in the possession of fishing poles."

Georgina smiled. Had Lord Greystone actually just made a joke? Who was this person?

She allowed herself to be led away. Greystone helped her down the slope, which was slippery with damp grass, guiding her down with strong arms.

He picked up the pole and said, "Now you will cast your line, doing your best not entangle it with Mr. Ledbridge's line, as he has had a terrible time already this morning."

Georgina laughed. She had never seen Lord Greystone this gay. Perhaps she had been wrong about his overly serious nature? It would not surprise her; she had found out recently that she was wrong about most things.

She took the pole, really having no idea of how to get started, and held it in front of her as if it were a live snake.

Lord Greystone stood behind her. His arms encircled her and moved her hands to the grip near the bottom of the pole. "There," he said, "now you shall just move it over your shoulder and cast it forward."

Georgina pulled the pole upright, shut her eyes and threw it forward. She peeked and saw the line had at least landed in the water.

"A good start," Lord Greystone said. "Now you must just wait to feel a tug, then you know you've got something."

"Lord Greystone," Miss Stanhope called. "Miss Hargrave and I require you to settle a dispute."

Georgina glanced up. Greystone looked annoyed. He turned to the girls and said, "Yes, of course." To Georgina he squeezed her hands and said, "Shall you be all right fishing alone?"

"I would assume so," she said laughing, "unless I catch a whale, in which case I shall drop the pole and run."

Greystone climbed the bank while Georgina wrestled with her pole, determined not to get caught in Mr. Ledbridge's line. She had smiled when Lord Greystone had been called away, but secretly she was most vexed with Miss Stanhope. Things had been going so well!

Who knew where their conversation might have gone if they had not been interrupted by that blond menace.

Georgina suddenly remembered what the Dowager had said about Miss Stanhope's bat ears and it cheered her up immensely. It also occurred to her that Greystone would be unlikely to take the same girl into dinner twice, it would be terribly bad form. That, she thought, might well leave Miss Stanhope out in the cold this evening.

As the hour wore on, Georgina had to admit that whatever else she thought of Miss Stanhope, the girl was a skilled predator. Georgina heard Lord Greystone try to escape more than once, only to be faced with another question he must settle. By the time Miss Stanhope was done with him, Mr. Ledbridge was helping Georgina up the slope. She had not caught anything, but she had not fallen in or broken the pole so, all in all, she felt her first fishing excursion was a success.

That evening, Georgina wore her dark blue silk. She thought it would set her apart from the other girls, who would be a parade of pastels. She hardly knew where to place herself in the drawing room. Should she stand near Lord Greystone so that she was handily nearby when it was time to go into dinner? Or would that make her look like a schemer? Should she stand far away, as if she did not care one way or another? Or would that make her look as if she did not care one way or another? She had spent years with piano instructors, drawing masters and dancing masters and, somehow, none of those people had ever mentioned where to stand in the drawing room under such circumstances.

As it happened, she needn't have fretted about it. Lord Greystone arrived late, moments before they were to go to dinner. He strode directly to her and said, "Miss Marksley, may I take you in?"

She held out her arm.

Lord Tansby once again escorted Ann. Georgina was afraid the poor fellow would declare himself and be turned down. He was certainly willing to risk bad manners in order to be Ann's escort for the second evening in a row. Miss Hastings-Bass was dreamily floating along on Lord Vanderman's arm and Sir Lewis led in Ms. Smith. Miss Templeton and Miss Cavendish escorted each other and seemed quite happy with the arrangement.

Lord Greystone led Georgina past a fuming Miss Stanhope.

After the first course was served, Greystone said, "It is not at all polite dinner conversation, but I think you will not mind if I mention the fever committees."

"Not at all," Georgina said.

"I've taken your counsel about drainage very seriously and have begun making improvements to the estate. It is my hope that my tenants suffer less disease because of it."

"I, too, have thought of it," Georgina said. "I am determined to convince my father to do the same, though how I will broach such a subject, I know not."

"I'm certain you will find a way. The people's health must take precedence over the embarrassment of the subject."

Ah, Georgina thought. There's a little of the old Greystone. A bit dictatorial. Yet, she found that she did not mind, for she thought he was quite unaware of it. His utmost concern was for the welfare of the people and his enthusiasm for the subject was evident.

"I really think," Georgina said, "that someone ought to write a pamphlet on the subject. It would not be suitable for me to do such a thing, but you might do it."

"A pamphlet?" Greystone said, considering the idea. "Yes, of course. Then every landowner in England could make the improvements."

Lord Greystone became engrossed with the scheme and talked at length on how it might be done, quite ignoring Miss Templeton on his left. Georgina noticed the Dowager eyeing them from the other end of the table.

Dinner passed by remarkably quickly. Lord Greystone said, "I must apologize for monopolizing the conversation. I should have been talking to you about the wine or the gardens or some other appropriate subject."

"Do not apologize," Georgina said. "It was a nice change to be discussing something so weighty, rather than the usual vacuous repartee. Rather like the difference between a meringue and a hearty stew."

Georgina thought that must have been the oddest thing she had ever said to a dinner partner, yet she felt she could say what truly occurred to her with Lord Greystone.

He smiled and said, "I would prefer a stew to a meringue any night."

The ladies retired to the drawing room, leaving the men to their cigars and port. The Dowager excused herself early, saying that as the girls had been thoroughly interviewed the night before, they might allow themselves to relax.

Lady Tennesby and Lady Worthington were left as chaperones. Georgina went to the pianoforte. She was so full of the conversation at dinner that she had no wish to make idle chatter. She played a simple tune that allowed her to think as she played.

How different it was to have a person genuinely interested in her ideas. She was all for pretty gowns and gloves and jewelry and all the fripperies of Bond Street. She liked nothing more than choosing the perfect little reticule or ribbon. And yet, there was something immensely gratifying about having this man listen to her thoughts. The carefully contrived picture she presented to the world, all smiles and silk, was what the world generally took her for. None of the young gentleman she had danced with over the season had asked her what she thought about anything more serious than the weather.

What would life be like with such a man? Georgina knew that many of her mother's acquaintance led nearly separate lives. They went forward as friendly strangers. She supposed that was bound to happen when the temperaments of the couple did not suit. She had been blessed with parents who shared genuine affection – her father respected and admired her mother above all else and she was the only one who could persuade him to put down his books or leave his club on occasion. They enjoyed each other's company every day when they were in the country. Could she have the same?

As Georgina had been daydreaming on the pianoforte, the gentlemen had come in and somebody had suggested a dance. Chairs were being moved out of the way and Miss Stanhope said loudly, "Miss Marksley must play. Her skill is unparalleled."

Georgina cursed herself for her inattention and for Miss Stanhope's slyness. Now, she would be stuck playing as the others danced. She sighed, there was nothing for it but to accept it with good grace. In a drawing room dance, someone always got stuck providing the music.

She struck up a lively country dance and peeked at the couples. Ann was paired with Lord Tansby, and looking rather alarmed about it. Georgina could guess that her cousin was headed for a difficult dilemma. If Lord Tansby asked for her hand, and Sir Langston as of yet had not, what was she to do? Turn down a Duke on the chance that Langston would ask? And what of Ann's parents? Georgina might well keep a secret from her own, but Ann could not. Would Ann's parents pressure her to accept Tansby? Georgina resolved to write to her mother and hint that Ann was unhappy. Her mother and Sir Langston were old friends, perhaps her mother would pass along the hint to him. There would be no reason to mention anything about Lord Tansby.

Georgina smiled as she played the keys. She was becoming a positive romantic. Just months ago, she would have pressed Ann to accept Tansby on account of his position.

The couples whirled by her and Georgina saw that Miss Stanhope had once more captured Lord Greystone. She began to feel uneasy. It was all well and good that Greystone admired her mind, but was he proof against Miss Stanhope's blond curls? In truth, she did not know.

Georgina ended the song and began thumbing through the sheet music in front of her, looking for something suitable. Ann tapped her shoulder. "I should like to take a turn, if you do not mind, Georgina."

Georgina looked at her cousin gratefully and squeezed her hand. She knew that Ann had volunteered solely for her benefit, as her cousin truly disliked playing in public.

Ann took her place and Georgina moved to the side of the drawing room. Lord Greystone bowed to Miss Stanhope and excused himself. He approached her and said, "I was afraid you might get caught at the pianoforte all evening. I see your cousin has kindly relieved you."

"Yes," Georgina said. "Ann is the kindest person I know."

"We must not let her kindness go to waste then," Lord Greystone said, holding out a hand.

Ann played a fast-paced Irish air. With so few couples to dance, Georgina was nearly breathless half way through the changes. Lord Greystone led her down the line with a steady arm. As she began her turn, skipping around the gentleman and watching the turquoise room flash by her in a blur, she thought she had never been happier.

The next day passed by blissfully. In the afternoon, there was a picnic by one of the lakes that bordered the house and the Dowager Countess had her footman wheel her to the spot. Lemonade and cold meats and cheeses were spread on a folding table and chairs were scattered about for everyone's comfort. Georgina gazed at the lake and thought there could not be a lovelier place on earth.

Dinner came and Lord Greystone escorted Miss Cavendish, but somehow contrived that Georgina was on his left. As Miss Cavendish had little to say, he was free to turn to Georgina often.

Georgina's hopes grew by the hour. Lord Greystone paid her marked attention when he was not being cornered by the clever Miss Stanhope. Georgina noticed that Miss Stanhope's smiles had become thin and her laughter brittle.

The following day was the ball and Georgina could hardly bear to think what would happen that evening. Was she seeing things as they were, or only how she wished them to be? Did he have the sort of feelings for her that would lead to a proposal, or did he merely enjoy conversing with her about drains? She felt as if she were walking through the world upside down – hardly able to comprehend all that was around her.

What if she were wrong? What if Lord Greystone walked off with Miss Stanhope? She could see Miss Stanhope's cunning clearly enough, but that did not mean he saw it. She was a great beauty, Georgina had to admit that, and might not the Earl want such a woman on his arm? What then?

Georgina recalled the Dowager's comment about how some of the girls would leave crying in their carriage. If Georgina were wrong, if what was between them was just interesting conversation, she would be one of them. Georgina pushed from her mind the image of Lady Tennesby watching her cry all the way back to London.

She tossed and turned throughout the night and fretted through most of the next day. Jemma struggled to get her ready for the ball. Her maid had already been to see Ann, and her cousin slipped in through the connecting door to see how she got on.

"Oh Georgina," Ann said, admiring her dress. "It is stunning."

Georgina gazed at her image. Once again, her mother had been right. Lady Marksley had chosen a white organza and had the seamstress sew red rosebuds along the bodice. The dress was springtime in a gown. The white set off Georgina's dark hair and her eyes had never looked so blue. She would have to remember to tell her mother that from now on, when it came to gowns, Georgina would trust in her mother's judgment implicitly.

"This should be quite an evening," Ann said.

"Truly," Georgina said. "Or quite a disaster."

"You love him, Georgina. I can see that. I believe he feels the same."

"Do you think it, truly?" Georgina asked.

"I do," Ann said resolutely.

Ann's answer gave her comfort. She knew her cousin would never give her a false answer on any subject, and particularly not on one this important. "I feel as if a hundred butterflies have taken flight inside me," Georgina said.

Ann smiled, but said nothing.

"And you, Ann?" Georgina said. "What shall you do if Lord Tansby proposes? He seems likely to."

Ann blushed. "He already has, and I have refused him."

Georgina held her hand up to stop Jemma fussing with her hair. "When? How?"

"He waylaid me this morning after breakfast as I was looking for a book in the library," Ann said. "He was very gracious toward my refusal. I know my father and mother will be very angry, but I am resolute in the matter."

Georgina turned to Ann. "I shall stand with you, cousin. Sir Langston does not know what a treasure he has in you, though he certainly shall once he gets around to asking for your hand."

"And if he does not, I shall be a spinster. But, I am decided. I will accept no one else. I feel very bold saying so, but there it is."

"And if all does not go well for me, Ann, I shall join you and we will live happily enough together in some small seaside town. We shall spend our days feeding the gulls and watching the waves come in."

"Good heavens," Ann said, laughing. "Let us pray it does not come to that."

Georgina had peeked into the darkened ballroom the day before. It had seemed a lonely, empty space. Now, it was lit with a hundred candles and footmen scurried to and fro, arranging chairs, directing the musicians and handing out glasses of champagne.

This was sure to be the oddest ball England had ever known. With nine girls and five gentlemen, at any given time four of the girls would sit out. That mattered little to Georgina. She knew that everything would be understood when Lord Greystone asked for the first dance. He could not dance with his choice all evening, that would be too rude, but he would certainly ask his choice for the first dance. The first dance was yards of silk and emeralds and diamonds, the rest of the dances were just ribbons and paste.

Lord Tansby, Mr. Ledbridge, Lord Vanderman and Sir Lewis had already entered the ballroom. It would have been usual for the gentleman to begin asking the ladies for dances, but they did not. Clearly, they did not know who Lord Greystone would choose for the first dance and did not want to interfere with his plans.

Georgina gazed around the ballroom. Lord Greystone had not yet made an appearance, nor had the Dowager. The rest of the guests looked on edge. Miss Stanhope stood as if she were nearly frozen in time, though Georgina had to admit the girl had never looked better. Her curls were done to perfection, shining under the light of the candles, and she wore a pale pink gown with yards of tulle overlay. She was like a confection one might find in the window of the finest French bakery.

Miss Cavendish and Miss Templeton looked silently alarmed. Georgina began to suspect that perhaps the two girls had suitors at home. It was true that they were never particularly chatty or gay, but at Greystone Hall they had been positively silent.

Miss Hargrave tried to put on a bold face, but was not particularly successful. Miss Hastings-Bass looked as a deer surrounded by hunters. Miss Smith fussed with her auburn hair and fidgeted. Only Miss Lennox and Ann appeared at all easy, and even they were not their usual serene selves.

Georgina knew she must appear just as fidgety. She had tugged at her gloves so many times she was surprised they were not shredded.

The butler gave a signal to the musicians and they began to tune their instruments. It would not be long now. Whatever was to be her fate – the happiest girl in the world, or crying in a carriage back to London – she would know it soon.

Everyone had turned toward the doors to the ballroom, staring at the empty space.

The Dowager appeared, and Lord Greystone pushing her chair. Georgina was surprised to note that he looked on edge himself. She had been solely focused on her own nerves, it had not occurred to her that this night would be just as fraught for the Earl.

Lord Greystone wheeled his mother to the side of the ballroom where she would have a good view of the dancers. He turned and looked at the faces surrounding him.

Georgina felt as if time had slowed. Everything and everyone appeared to be moving in slow motion.

His eyes met hers. She knew she should look away, as a demonstration of modesty, but she stared at him boldly. There was no time for feminine wiles. Either this man would ask her or he would not, but she would be sure to let him know how she viewed the matter.

Lord Greystone smiled, looking slightly relieved. He approached her and bowed.

Georgina curtsied, willing herself to stay on her feet.

"Miss Marksley," he said, "may I have the first dance?"

Chapter Thirteen

There he was, Lord Greystone at the ball, asking her for the first dance. She gazed up into his stormy grey eyes, which now that she had taken to staring at him, she noticed were flecked with blue. "Yes," she said.

Georgina was vaguely aware of what went on around her. The other gentleman quickly asked partners. Miss Stanhope, left standing at the side of the dance floor, flounced out of the ballroom. The music began.

Georgina and Lord Greystone were silent as they moved through the changes, there seemed little that needed to be said. Toward the end of the dance, Lord Greystone whispered close in her ear, "May I speak with you in private sometime before we go into supper?"

"Yes," Georgina said. She smiled. So far this night, all she had said to Lord Greystone was yes and yes. She intended to keep saying yes to all his questions.

The dance ended and Lord Greystone led her to a chair and handed her a glass of champagne. Georgina knew he could not ask her to dance the second, nor with this few gentlemen on hand, could he choose to sit out.

"I would rather sit," he said, "but…"

"But duty," Georgina said.

"Exactly." Lord Greystone glanced around the room. He approached Ann and asked her for the dance. Georgina felt it was thoughtfully done and meant to put her mind at ease. He knew they were cousins and close cousins at that. There was no question of there being anything between Ann and the Earl.

The dance began and Georgina turned and gazed out onto the balcony. The doors had been thrown open to admit the crisp night air into the ballroom. She would not see Greystone again until the six dances were through and it was near time for the supper. But then, then he would ask.

She stepped out onto the slate stones, the coolness seeping through her slippers. The balcony bordered the gravel drive and Georgina marveled at how the little stones reflected the moonlight. The night sky was glorious, a big dark pincushion stuck with a hundred sparkling diamonds. How lucky she was! She had made so many mistakes, and yet somehow she was standing here in this moment.

Georgina walked the length of the balcony, trying to compose herself for her interview with Lord Greystone.

She was suddenly grabbed from behind, rough arms pinning her arms against her sides. "Shush, Georgina," the man said, "it's me."

"Edmund!"

"Come quickly," he said. "Your mother is ill and I fear she has not long for this world."

As he said it, Edmund pushed her along to the steps at the side of the balcony. Georgina's mind raced. "My mother! But what has happened?"

"She's ill, now hurry," Edmund said.

A carriage waited in the dark part of the drive where the lights from the ballroom did not reach.

"But wait," Georgina cried, "I must fetch Ann, and pack and make my excuses to the Dowager!"

Edmund had thrust her into the carriage. "There's no time," he said. "I'll send a carriage for Ann and your maid tomorrow, you may write the Dowager and tell her what has happened."

Edmund slammed the door and the coachman barreled down the drive.

"But what has happened, Edmund? My mother was in fine health just days ago. How could she fall ill so suddenly?"

Georgina sat back. She suddenly knew. Fever. While she had been enjoying herself in the country, fever had swept through the city. How could she have thought she was so clever to outwit it? As if a few drain improvements could stop the fever.

"It is the fever, is it not?"

Edmund looked distracted and peered back toward Greystone Hall. "Yes, that's it," he said.

The coach arrived at the gates and the coachman shouted at the gatekeeper to hurry up about it. The old man swung the gates open and jumped out of the way of the oncoming horses.

The carriage swung to the right and raced down the darkened lane. Georgina froze. The coach was going the wrong way. London was the other way. She remembered it clearly enough when they had arrived.

"Edmund," she said cautiously, "your coachman has gone in the wrong direction."

Edmund did not answer her. Now that her eyes began to adjust to the darkened carriage, she saw he was ghostly white and his eyes were bloodshot. Then she remembered that Edmund had been sent home to the country. He had not been in London. He had not been with her mother.

"Edmund," she said in a low tone, "my mother is not ill, is she?"

"Of course she is," he said hurriedly.

Georgina could see he was lying. She should have seen it when he caught her on the balcony, but it had all happened so fast.

Edmund drank from a flask.

"Tell me," Georgina said. "Tell me what you are doing."

Edmund did not answer. Georgina lunged for the door handle. She would throw herself out of the carriage and run back to Greystone Hall.

Edmund grasped her wrists in a vice-like grip. "That's enough!" he said.

Georgina struggled against him. "You will let me go, Edmund. You will let me go right now!"

"I will not," Edmund muttered. He tied her wrists together with rope brought out from his waistcoat pocket.

"You are kidnapping me against my will?" she cried.

After finding he had cheated at cards, Georgina had viewed Edmund badly enough, but she had never imagined anything like this. "I will shout to the coachman," she said.

"Go ahead," Edmund said in a vicious tone. "The man has been paid well and he knows what we're about."

"What? What is it we're about? What possible ending can this have?"

Edmund snorted. "The best possible ending, my girl. We shall be husband and wife."

Georgina felt ice settle into her veins. She saw it all now. Edmund would have her dowry one way or another. Still, he could not force her to marry. Not even in Gretna Green would he find anyone to marry an unwilling girl.

"I will not marry you," she said sternly. "I am shortly to be engaged to Lord Greystone. At least, I think I am. I believe he plans to propose this very night."

Edmund's face became contorted in fury. "Greystone," he said, his voice full of hate. "Greystone will not want you after this night."

Georgina thought about that. Would Lord Greystone really believe she had gone off with Edmund willingly? No, she did not think so. A month ago, perhaps. But not now.

It slowly dawned on her what Edmund really meant. How he planned to force her to marry. He would take her honor, and then she would have no choice but to fly to Gretna Green.

Chapter Fourteen

"I will never let you do it, you base creature," she hissed at Edmund, struggling with the rope around her wrists. "You are a spoiled little boy, and no match for me."

Edmund seemed taken aback by her fury.

Georgina herself was shocked. She had never been so angry. She would not allow Edmund to ruin her life. She simply would not allow it. She gave in to her rage.

"And even if you ruin me," she said, "and force me to marry you, you would spend the rest of your days looking over your shoulder, wondering when I might poison you or plunge a dagger through your heart while you sleep. And rest assured, cousin, I'd do it."

Edmund slapped her hard. Georgina was momentarily speechless.

"Stop talking!" he shouted. "It's too late. I cannot get by without your dowry and that's that. If my stupid sister had done as I asked and helped me, I would not have had to go to all this trouble. Listen here," he said, "I'm not going to be made uncomfortable just because a silly girl has an opinion. You'll do as your told. As for afterward, there will be no opportunity to poison me as I will be living in London and you will live on the estate."

Georgina's breath caught. This was not some rash adventure, thought up suddenly. Edmund had planned out the future. Where was he taking her? To some seedy little inn? Or perhaps he had rented a house in some lonely place.

Edmund looked as if he had gone mad. Perhaps he had. If she would have any chance of escape, she must think clearly and calmly.

"Now Edmund," she said softly, "surely you do not want to do this. Simply turn around now and all will be forgiven."

"Shut up!" Edmund shouted. "I do not need your forgiveness. I have a right!"

Georgina did not know how her cousin thought he had a right, but she could see that it was hopeless to reason with him. He drank more and more from his flask, and she thought her only chance might be if he were to pass out.

The miles rolled by as they passed lonely farmhouses. Georgina silently worked on the ropes around her wrists, stealing glances at Edmund from time to time. His eyes were only half open.

The rope around her wrists finally loosened and she slipped one wrist out. She could see the lights of a farmhouse ahead. This was her chance. Georgina freed her other wrist and lunged for Edmund's flask. She tore it from his hands and threw the brandy into his face.

Edmund cried out and clutched at his eyes, temporarily blinded. Georgina banged on the ceiling of the carriage, hard, hoping the coachman would assume it was Edmund who gave the command to halt.

The carriage slowed and Georgina leapt down to the road before it rolled to a stop. Edmund staggered out behind her. "Get back in the carriage, Georgina," he said.

Georgina pushed him away, desperate to get to the farmhouse they had just passed. Edmund grasped her tighter as his vision began to clear.

Edmund shouted to the coachman, "Do not just sit there, you imbecile, come down and help me!"

The coachman peered down at them. He shook his head and said, "I was just to take a young couple to Gretna Green. Nothing was said about the girl bein' unwilling."

Georgina heard the sound of distant hoof beats. Praise God it was someone who could help her, some sturdy farmer or even a highwayman.

Edmund heard it too, and began to force her back to the carriage. Georgina broke free and ran toward the sound.

A black figure emerged down the lane and galloped toward her. Georgina was swept off her feet and into the saddle. Strong arms encircled her as the horse passed the carriage and slowed.

"Are you hurt?"

Greystone. It was Lord Greystone.

"But how--" she exclaimed.

"Never mind that now," Greystone said, turning his horse. "Can you keep your seat?"

Georgina nodded.

Greystone trotted back to the carriage. He leapt down from his horse. The coachman cried, "I didn't know nothin' about the girl bein' unwilling!"

Greystone ignored him and walked toward Edmund.

Edmund stood straight and said boldly, "You're too late, Greystone. I've taken her honor and now we must be married."

Lord Greystone stared at Edmund. Georgina was on the verge of shouting that it was not true.

"Do not be ridiculous," Greystone said, and punched Edmund in the jaw.

Edmund hit the ground, and stayed there.

Greystone ordered the coachman to help him tie Edmund up and dump him in the carriage. Georgina watched her cousin being pitched in unceremoniously, head first. The coachman was directed to follow them back to Greystone Hall, where the magistrate would be called.

Lord Greystone mounted his horse behind Georgina, wrapping his arms around her. "Are you certain you can ride?" he asked.

"Quite," she answered.

"Then we shall go slowly," he said, moving his stallion to a walk. "We have much to talk about."

Georgina leaned back in his arms. Where she had felt terrified of Edmund, she felt safe with Greystone. Clever man, to come to her rescue. But how in the world did he do it?

"First," he said, "I would like to imagine that we are just about to go in for supper."

"Ah, yes," Georgina said. "You wished to speak with me."

"I did. I do. What I mean to say is, Miss Marksley…"

"Georgina," she said.

"Yes. Georgina. Will you do me the honor of becoming my wife?"

This was not at all how Georgina had thought a proposal would come about. On horseback, riding down a darkened lane with her cousin shouting expletives from the carriage. Yet, it all seemed perfect somehow. Thanks to Edmund, she knew that come what may, Greystone would be there to catch her from falling.

"Yes," she said.

They rode along in happy silence. Then Georgina said, "How did you know to come after me? How did you discover what had happened?"

"Ah," he said, "you can thank your cousin for that. She noticed you were not in the ballroom, as had I. I did not suspect anything, I thought perhaps you were freshening your hair or whatever it is that young ladies do when they disappear."

Georgina laughed. "Yes," she said, "I suppose the disappearances might well seem mysterious to a man."

"Very," Lord Greystone said. "Your cousin went to your room to see if you were well. As she was walking down the hall, she observed Miss Stanhope coming from your room. Miss Stanhope made some excuse of being confused and walking into the wrong room. Miss Carrington believed her, until she entered the room and found a note. It said you had run off with Edmund Carrington to Gretna Green and asked that no one follow you. Your cousin instantly recognized the handwriting as being her brother's, not your own."

"But what has Miss Stanhope got to do with it?"

"She was questioned by my mother," Lord Greystone continued, "and confessed all. Miss Stanhope's brother is a crony of Edmund Carrington's and the three schemed together. Miss Stanhope had set her cap on me and Carrington had set his cap on you. Miss Stanhope was only too happy to assist your cousin with his plan. That is why she had entered your room. She placed the note."

"Oh my," Georgina said. "I saw her leave the ballroom before the first dance. I suppose that is where she was going."

"No matter," Lord Greystone said. "Where Miss Stanhope is going at the moment is to the nearest inn under the watchful eye of Lady Worthington. Once my mother heard all, she had the little miss packed up and out the door in minutes."

Georgina watched the moon shining down from the sky. It was a beautiful moon, and it was a beautiful night. Nothing could have been more perfect.

"And to think," she murmured, "Miss Stanhope's scheme might have worked. After all, those blond curls might be hard to resist."

Lord Greystone laughed. "I see you still did not discover the ruse. Miss Stanhope never had a hope of success."

"What ruse?" Georgina asked.

"The summons," Lord Greystone said. "I was the author of that scheme, not my mother. After our conversation in the conservatory I knew I would have little chance to ever win your heart. I felt I needed to have my little sprite captured on my estate for a week to have any chance at all. That very night of the Prince's ball, after you so skillfully verbally trounced me, I set off to Greystone Hall. The following day, I had a conference with my mother. She was quite amused by the whole idea and entreated Lady Tennesby to set the whole thing up."

Georgina blushed at the mention of her outburst in the conservatory. "But you see," she said, "I did not know--"

"Yes," he said. "I know."

"I nearly died when I discovered that Lady Tennesby had composed the list of girls," she said. "I thought that meant--"

"Lady Tennesby did not compose the list. I did. Though Lady Tennesby has been in on the truth of it since the beginning."

"Oh," Georgina said. "You see, she told me while we were traveling here that she had decided which girls to invite."

"Yes," Greystone said laughing, "she told my mother and I that she had done so. I could have guessed as much when I saw the look on your face when I entered the drawing room on the day of your arrival."

"And what would you have done, sir, if I had not come?"

"Ah, that. That was the one rub in the mix. I thought I might claim a terrible illness and send everyone back to London. You see, when I first saw you in Hyde Park, as idiotic as I appeared, I was struck by your beauty. But it was in the supper room at Almack's that I knew you must be mine. Here was a pretty girl, very pretty I might add, who cared something for her fellow man. You had clearly thought about how to help, and that meant something to me. I have been through enough seasons to have become, I'm embarrassed to admit, somewhat jaded about the fairer sex."

Georgina began to fear that Lord Greystone did not understand her real nature. He seemed to think she was some sort of saint. She felt she had better be as honest with him as she had been with the Dowager, as he was bound to find her out. "Lord Greystone--"

"Henry," he said.

"Henry. I must tell you, you deserve to know the truth, I am not nearly so good a person as you think, not nearly as good as you are. I've told your mother all about it, and no doubt she will acquaint you with it."

"Nonsense," Lord Greystone said. "We are of different natures, that is true. You are full of high spirits and I am Lord Gloomy."

Georgina started. "Where did you ever--"

"Miss Stanhope overheard you call me Lord Gloomy at one of the Almack's committee meetings. She was only too happy to tell me."

"But, oh, she should not have…"

"She certainly should not have, though that and a few other comments allowed me to see her true character long ago. Of course, I was angry when I heard it. But, over time, I realized I was angry because it was true. I shall count on you to lighten my spirits and scold me terribly whenever I am being particularly Lord Gloomy."

"Then you must promise to gloom me down a bit when my high spirits are running too high."

"Never," he said, firmly.

They had turned in the gate and over the crest of the hill. Greystone Hall loomed ahead, lit up against the night sky. "Now," Lord Greystone said, "we shall see my mother. She has been watching you with interest this past week and is already very fond of you. Afterward, I shall write to your father and ask for an audience and send it with my fastest man. I shall follow my man in the morning and see your father immediately."

Entering the ballroom, Georgina realized she was a mess. Her gown was torn and muddied and she seemed to have lost one of her slippers. Before she could protest that she must get changed, Lord Greystone steered her through the gaping guests to his mother's chair.

Georgina curtsied.

"Well, girl," the Dowager Countess said, "It seems there is no end of lengths a gentleman will go to secure your hand."

Georgina blushed, but she could see that the Dowager was not at all vexed. Her bright eyes sparkled with amusement.

"When my son informed me that he would need a week long house party to woo you, I thought it quite astonishing. But also one of the most diverting things I've heard in ages."

The Dowager turned to her son and said, "Well? Have you done it?"

Lord Greystone bowed. "I have."

"And all is well?" she asked.

"Very well," Lord Greystone said.

"Excellent," she said. "Now we are quite late for supper and cook will be fuming below stairs. You may want to change, Miss Marksley."

Georgina curtsied. As she turned to leave the ballroom, Ann rushed to her side. "Oh Georgina," she said. "I am so sorry."

Georgina hugged her cousin. "Why ever for, dear Ann? I am engaged."

Edmund had been taken by the footmen and secured in the stables for the night. Lord Greystone, having had the night to think about it, decided not to call the magistrate. After all, as much as he might dislike it, he would be forever related to the future Viscount.

Early the following morning, Lord Greystone paid a visit to the barn. Georgina never discovered what was said, but Edmund was given a horse and escorted off the property. Georgina saw that he was shaken as he rode away and did not think he would trouble her again.

When Georgina arrived home after two long days of traveling, she found that Greystone had already been to see her father and approval had been given. Lady Marksley liked to say that she had known all along that it would be Lord Greystone of the stormy eyes.

Ann was surprised to find Sir Langston waiting for her when she arrived in London. He wasted no time dropping to one knee and securing her hand. It turned out Lady Marksley had indeed taken Georgina's hint in the letter she wrote and passed along the hint to Sir Langston. Fearing he had waited too long to make his intentions known, he had ridden up to London on his fastest horse.

Ann had been terrified that her parents would be angry with her for refusing Lord Tansby, but as it happened, Ann's father had thought Ann coming to London for the season would be all for naught as he had quite settled on Sir Langston. They had become friendly and Sir Carrington thought Sir Langston a very pleasant fellow to invite for a shooting party.

Months later, Georgina became the Countess of Knightsbridge. The wedding took place at St. George's, with Ann at her side as the maid of honor. Prinny acted as best man.

The Dowager made a special trip to town for the event as she had grown inordinately fond of Georgina. Georgina had thought the wedding breakfast would be quiet and confined to the families, but the Dowager announced that she had not made such a long journey to forgo a party. The breakfast was a lavish affair held at Greystone's house in town. It seemed all of London was there, with the exception of Miss Stanhope and Edmund Carrington.

After Ann and Sir Langston were married, they became frequent visitors to Greystone Hall, where they found Georgina just as high-spirited as ever, but Lord Greystone far less gloomy.

The End

If you liked *A Summons to Greystone Hall*, please write a review at the following the link: http://www.amazon.com/Summons-Greystone-clean-regency-romance-ebook/dp/B01A65QJNK/ref=sr_1_1?s=digital-text&ie=UTF8&qid=1451950037&sr=1-1

If you would like to get notice of the next Perpetua Langley release, join her mailing list at: http://eepurl.com/bLESdf.

Perpetua will only send email notifications of new releases or free chapters and novellas. Perpetua never sends spam and does not sell her lists.

Printed in Great Britain
by Amazon